"I think you've earned a trial period," Ford mused

"But you may have to do better if you want to stay permanently."

"Just say yes or no, Mr. Barron," Briony said tartly. "If there's any question of my paying for my job in a physical way, I'll pack right now."

"You paid a minute ago, quite willingly, I thought. However, I was referring to your other performance—" The flame-blue eyes flicked contemptuously around the neglected garden. "From what I see you haven't been doing a great deal."

"In that case," Briony snapped, "you can be assured that on your next visit you'll be completely satisfied."

He smiled. "I see you've grasped the situation," he murmured. "That's exactly what I expect. To be completely satisfied."

Books by Ann Charlton

HARLEQUIN ROMANCE

These books may be available at your local bookseller.

Don't miss any of our special offers. Write to us at the following address for information on our newest releases.

Harlequin Reader Service
P.O. Box 52040, Phoenix, AZ 85072-2040
Canadian address: P.O. Box 2800, Postal Station A,
5170 Yonge St., Willowdale, Ont. M2N 6J3

No
Last Song

Ann Charlton

Harlequin Books

TORONTO • NEW YORK • LONDON
AMSTERDAM • PARIS • SYDNEY • HAMBURG
STOCKHOLM • ATHENS • TOKYO • MILAN

Original hardcover edition published in 1984
by Mills & Boon Limited

ISBN 0-373-02684-6

Harlequin Romance first edition April 1985

CHAPTER ONE

BRIONY WILDE was centre stage when the first spotlight flared. She was caught in its glare, her costumed figure like some fantasy fugitive as she hastily moved back into shadow.

But she had been noticed and the small group of people, lingering for the band's opening number, were drawn across the grass-clumped ground to the overspilling light.

The man had noticed, too.

Briony had seen his face turn towards her as she stood there—his eyes had trapped her as surely as the spotlight. It was the second time tonight she had felt him watching.

The air was chill and Briony wrapped her arms about herself as she looked out over the coloured lights and stalls of the charity Gala Fête. It was expertly set up in the grounds of someone's country estate. The house itself was some little distance from the marquee and bazaars. All that could be seen of it in the gathering dusk were the lights near the entrance throwing leafy shadows on mellow, old brick.

Her eyes came back to the people near the stage and her stomach growled as she watched a girl devour a hamburger. A little apart from the crowd the tall man bent his head to listen to a woman before he moved away with her in the direction of the stalls. But he glanced once more at the stage before he went.

'Who is he?' Briony grabbed Jeff's sleeve as he came up beside her with the band's glittering sign. He shaded his eyes and looked out at the two people.

'They're on the charity committee running this do. His name is—oh—Barry, something like that. Why?'

'He keeps looking at—up here.' She didn't think she'd imagined it. Those keen eyes hadn't merely been inspecting the stage—they'd been inspecting her.

Jeff grinned and ran his eyes up and down her slim figure. 'You do look rather eyecatching, love.'

'I didn't say he was looking at me.' Briony felt uncomfortable at the thought, though it was surprising that she should. She'd been the focus of an audience's attention countless times and was used to it.

'No. You didn't *say* that.'

'How come you always know what I'm thinking?' she asked in mock annoyance.

'Just a knack. A woman's mind is an open book to me.'

'Ha,' Briony said, then sighed. 'Maybe I was imagining him staring. But I'm a bit jumpy tonight.'

'Jumpy? You? Never.'

'Well it *is* three years since I was a band regular, Jeff. I'm a bundle of nerves.'

Jeff beckoned the road crew forward as they lumbered on stage with one of the six-foot-high speakers. 'Nerves you may have—but you haven't lost your touch, Bry. Your guitar work's great and you slipped into those vocal harmonies nice and easy.' His hazel eyes, so like her own, tilted at the corners as he grinned at her. 'The guys gave me a rough time when I told them my sister was filling in for Paul—and Cheryl.'

'I'll bet,' she said dryly.

'Watch that step,' Jeff called to Ritchie who was staggering with his drum kit. 'Your first rehearsal won them over though. Just one thing, Bry,' he dropped his arm about her shoulder, 'I know you like to sing soft and pretty at Rocco's but give us a bit of bite tonight, hey? A touch of Quatro, like you used to do.'

She wrinkled her nose but nodded. The 'touch of Quatro' was what had almost ruined her voice altogether and one of the reasons she had left Jeff's first real band. Briony watched him stand up the sign with its silver letters spelling out the name of his latest group. Silverhero. Only twenty-four, Jeff and been forming and reforming bands since he was sixteen. She had been in his first two—a modest folk trio and then in his first rock band, Rivals. But she had left it three years ago to study classical guitar. Nowadays she played mostly for her own ears, and for the customers at Rocco's coffee lounge twice a week, more for the pleasure of it than the pay.

Silverhero was Jeff's latest assembly of talent and a likeable bunch, Briony thought, smiling at Mike whose grin gleamed at her through a dense beard. They were all rather hairy. Ritchie with his handlebar moustache and Jeff with his shoulder-length hair. Paul, whose guitar she would play tonight, had a steel wool crop that looked like a hairdresser's creation but wasn't. Her eyes fell on Duane. A very nice bunch—with one exception. The brilliant lead guitarist returned her look with his insolent air and she moved closer to Jeff.

'Don't worry about Duane, Bry,' Jeff murmured in that disconcerting way he had. 'I'll be watching him. I always do.'

But would watching be enough, Briony wondered uneasily. From her first rehearsal last week Duane had leered at her even as his girlfriend Cheryl had smouldered. The band's regular singer was understandably angry at his wandering attention—with her face swollen and discoloured from a dental operation. Briony was doubling up—playing rhythm guitar instead of Paul while he played best man at a wedding—and singing instead of Cheryl. But not even Briony's coldest manner seemed to persuade Duane that she was replacing his girlfriend only as a singer tonight.

Finally satisfied with the positioning of the sign, Jeff shrugged his tartan jacket off and slipped it about her shoulders.

'You look chilly, Bry,' he grinned, anticipating her reaction.

'And who wouldn't be in this silly get-up,' she responded. 'I know this superhero stuff is Cheryl's trademark, but I don't know why you insisted on me wearing it. It doesn't even fit properly.' She looked down at the sequinned top and the brief shorts that made up the costume. They were bad enough, but worn with boots and her dark hair crimped and voluminous about her shoulders, she looked like a refugee from a comic strip.

'It's our trademark, too, now love, that's why. Cheryl did a good job on your hair.' He eyed the dark mane that framed her fine-boned face.

'Yes,' Briony said gloomily. 'I thought she might crimp my face as well—she glowered at me the whole time as if it was my fault her boyfriend keeps eyeing me. And I've never given him any encouragement.'

'You worry too much. Men are bound to eye you off. We're made that way—brutes, all of us.' He dodged the quick movement of her elbow, laughing softly. 'You mightn't stretch the gear to its limit like our Cheryl, but you've got a certain style—"Wilde" style. Remember how many fans you had in Rivals?'

'Yes, I certainly do,' she said dryly, 'and I'm glad to say that my fans at Rocco's never give me any trouble at all.'

'Neither did the others—not for long anyway. Speaking of—er—trouble, are you still seeing Martin-with-the-hands Thingammy?'

'Don't you ever remember a name? And no, I'm not seeing him. We—didn't see eye to eye about a few things as you know and called it off. And I've been too worried about finding a job for dating as it happens.'

'Bry,' Jeff began and she sighed, wishing she hadn't brought the subject up again, 'about tonight. I'm not happy about leaving you at the Stocklea pub after the show. Why not drive back to Sydney with us? You can't be serious about wanting this job as a gardener?'

And to be truthful, she couldn't offer any concrete reasons for wanting to do such a peculiar thing, other than the obvious ones—she was out of a job, had no car and needed some cheaper accommodation than Sydney could offer. A city girl all her life, she had felt an overpowering yen for the country when she'd read the newspaper advertisement:

'General gardening duties on large allotment. Quiet, restful surroundings. On-site caravan accommodation for suitable applicant. Apply Stocklea 5879. A. Gordon.'

It was the 'quiet, restful surroundings' that did it. The

words made images of still, sunny days—of air that smelled of new-mown grass and roses.

She found herself dwelling on it while she continued to apply for office jobs and turn up for temporary work. While her savings dwindled. While buses and trains carried her into the deafening city noise and home again to the flat that clattered with every passing train. 'You know very well that I want the job, Jeff. I wouldn't have agreed to fill in for you tonight except that the band was playing so close to Stocklea. It seemed like fate.'

'Fate! If you get the job, how on earth do you think you'd manage gardening duties?' He looked scornfully at her slim build. 'And what do you know about it, anyway?'

'Gardening's just a question of cutting off the right bits. And I used to do the McPherson's rose pruning—and the lawn.' She wrinkled her nose, aware that her experience was limited to say the least. One year of pruning roses and cutting grass in exchange for cheap board and lodgings with the dear old McPherson couple hardly fitted her to apply for the job. A wave of nostalgia hit her when she thought of those uncomplicated days. How come, she thought, that she could be in a bigger financial mess at twenty-two than she'd ever managed in her teens?

'Good God. You're not going to quote the McPherson experience are you? That was ages ago. And you told me yourself that poor old Pop McPherson could hardly see the grass at all and his wife was happy as long as she had a vase full of flowers in the lounge room. Critical employers they weren't.'

Briony sniffed in mock offence. 'Nevertheless, I visited them in their home unit and obtained a glowing reference. In these hard times of unemployment one must use every skill one has—and every contact.'

'You would have been better off using your skills to avoid old Groves' attention. I still say you needn't have given up a good job just because he made a mild sort of a pass at you.'

Briony grimaced. She had come to the same conclusion. 'That's alright for you. You're a boy.'

'*Man*—if you don't mind.'

She regarded him affectionately. '*Boy*. And as a boy, you don't have to work overtime with one eye on the boss to make sure he's not about to manoeuvre you into a corner.'

'Coward. You needn't have resigned.'

'He had bad breath,' she said reflectively and Jeff laughed.

'Oh well—if he had bad breath. . . .'

'But I wasn't a coward as it happened. I told him to stop patting my arm and he wasn't very pleasant after that. A resignation was really the only thing left. But I couldn't have picked a worse time to be on the job market.'

'True. But, Bry—a gardener! Can things be that bad?' He shook his head. 'Not that I think you'll get the job. One look at your lovely but far from robust form and Mrs Whatsername will laugh into her warm milk.'

'Warm milk?'

'You did say she was an oldie, didn't you?'

'She sounded elderly,' Briony said in a reproving tone, 'which is all to the good. I get on well with old people. And don't be too sure about me not getting the job. Mrs Gordon told me on that phone that she'd had no other applicants.'

'Aha. The odds are in your favour then, Bry.'

She could do with something in her favour, Briony thought. Things wouldn't have been so bad if it hadn't been for the car. Innocently parked at the kerb one day, it was demolished by a truck which vanished into thin air, witnessed by a lady with poor eyesight. The insurance company pointed out a tiny clause on her policy and refused to pay. The hire purchase company pointed out one on theirs and demanded the payments as usual. She gritted her teeth, posted off the car instalments and collected a bus timetable.

'Trouble always comes in threes,' their mother had often said and Briony crossed her fingers against any third event. But she'd lost a job and a car—there wasn't much left to lose.

'Are you okay for money?' Jeff asked suddenly.

'Of course.' Her smile was full of confidence. 'Ritchie wants you,' she prompted as he hesitated. If Jeff only knew just how close to penury she was, he might feel obliged to pay back the loan she had made him in her more affluent days. And Briony knew that that would mean selling off a piece of equipment just when the band was on the brink of success—a contract for a country tour.

Jeff left her and she hugged his jacket around her and closed her eyes against the vision conjured up by the smell of hamburgers and onions that drifted from one of the stalls. A big, fat, toasted roll—she thought—buttered and ozzing tomato sauce down its sides, and in the middle a succulent, savoury burger with salad that would slide out the sides when you took a bite. . . .

'Here—stop drooling and eat this.' Mike slapped a wilting chocolate bar into her hand, and she opened her eyes to his toothy smile—marooned in the wilderness of his beard. He patted his ample waist and ignored her protests. 'Better you than me—it might look harmless enough but the minute I swallowed it, it would become flab.' He flicked her mass of hair with one finger as he passed.

'Thanks, Mike,' she called after him, just as the second spotlight was switched on.

A movement below caught her eye and Briony recognised the same man again. He was nearer and she was able to meet his eyes directly. A small shiver ran down her back. She pulled Jeff's tartan jacket closer around her as if it might protect her—though from what she couldn't say. He showed no real expression, not even when she gave a polite smile. 'On the committee' Jeff had said and the man looked the kind who might be in charge of the whole thing. Tall and in his thirties she judged, he had the look of someone used to giving orders. Something to do with his arrogant posture gave that impression. He was looking up—yet managing to look down. One of the lights went out as the boys tested the outlets, plugging and unplugging each one in turn.

The man stood a moment longer, his face shadowed

theatrically. The strong line of his nose seemed almost hawk-like above a mouth made sensual by the play of light. But the spot came on again and Briony saw the expression of distaste on his thin lips before he turned away. She moved into the shadows at the back of the stage and watched his broad-shouldered figure pass the marquee. No doubt he was doing his rounds to make sure that everything ran smoothly.

The carousel whirled, its mirrored panels blinking back the glow of the fair in a multi-coloured heliograph. A third chorus of 'The Loveliest Night of the Year' waltzed with the fairy-tale horses that rose and dipped on their fluted poles. People thronged the aisles between the marquee and stalls and the hum of voices and laughter carried to the stage.

The man disappeared in the crowd. Briony looked down at the chocolate bar, mangled in her hand.

'Trouble always comes in threes. . . .' She shook herself. How stupid to let a strange man's disapproval bother her. He was the wrong age group for rock-and-roll and probably hated pop music. That was all. She looked down at herself again, felt the alien texture of her hair as she pushed it back and wryly admitted that she looked a trifle weird even by her own fairly tolerant standards. Maybe he thought she was a 'groupie'— hanging about in a provocative get-up with a man's jacket around her.

Duane brushed by, carrying his guitar in its velvet-lined case with the reverence he reserved for it alone.

'Centrefold stuff, darling,' he muttered and subjected her to one of his overheated looks. Briony reddened. As if it wasn't enough to have that—that—hawk-faced man appraising her as if she was some dubious piece of goods. Her anger was quite ridiculously out of proportion and she knew it.

'I'm sure you'd know, Duane. But then I imagine you always choose your reading matter for the pictures.'

Ritchie laughed and Duane's dark eyes narrowed. His lack of formal education was a sensitive area and Briony's thrust had gone home more cruelly than she intended. She marched off, conscious of Duane's sullen look and sorry that she had not simply ignored him as usual. The chocolate bar assuaged in part the gnawings in her stomach, but did nothing at all for the new, nervous flutterings that were there.

'Time,' Jeff said and she took off the jacket and put it in her bag, making the movements deliberate, slow. Even so, her hands shook a little as she picked up the heavy guitar, looped the neckstrap over her head and adjusted the tone and volume controls. The long lead snaked out across the stage with the others and she cleared it from her feet. Panicking she turned to Jeff where he stood at the keyboards. She couldn't even remember the opening chords of the first number ... but as all the spotlights flooded the stage and the crowd quietened, her former professionalism returned.

Her fingers found the chords automatically, the strings vibrated and she slid into the solid rhythm of an old Eagles number with a surge of excitement. A few people near the front began to clap their hands and Briony saw a grey-haired woman put her hands over her ears and say something to the man next to her. The volume was certainly high, but how high Briony could not tell from up here where the sound was relayed to them through the smaller speakers on stage facing them. But she could feel the floor vibrate underfoot with Mike's bass guitar and the drum beat.

Her dark hair flew about her face as she moved to the microphone to sing, then let her hands drop for four bars of Duane's brilliant lead. Her nerves were singing with the beat. But this was different from all those other times when she'd stood like this before a sea of faces. In the brief break she realised why.

There were over two hundred people out there and Briony knew exactly where the man was. She couldn't see him. If she could see him it wouldn't be so extraordinary ... she could feel him watching and she almost fumbled her cue so strong was the signal she was receiving. At least now he would know she wasn't just a groupie if that was the reason for his disdain. She wondered just what he thought of a costumed girl singing and toting a guitar. Her smile widened. With

the zany glitter eyeshadow, kohl liner and her full
mouth glossed, she looked no more than seventeen. Or
so Jeff had told her. 'A sensational seventeen' he'd
added to mollify her.

Maybe, she thought, that was what bothered the tall
man who looked so stern. Perhaps he thought she was
under age. His face materialised from all the others
suddenly and Briony held on to her smile with
difficulty. She dragged her eyes away from him,
wondering just why his attention should make her so
uneasy. Uneasier even than the way a few leather-
jacketed boys at the front were staring and loudly
commenting between numbers. But they were just kids
and didn't create the confusion within her that the dark
man did.

He had a woman with him, Briony noticed when her
eyes inevitably went back to him. His wife probably. He
was very likely a nice man—an accountant—or a bank
manager who took his charity work seriously and had
two or three kids wandering about with sticky candy-
floss faces.

The first half of their act wound up. Briony let her
hands relax as the closing bars faded to a riff played by
Duane. The loose ends of his guitar strings, sprouting
from the tuning pegs, splayed and shimmered silver in
their own rhythm. Duane looked like the devil in his all-
black clothes but there was no denying it—he played
like an angel.

As the crowd clapped, Jeff gave her the thumbs up
sign and she smiled as she lifted the strap from her neck
and looked about for somewhere safe to stand Paul's
guitar while they stopped for a break. The comments of
the youths who had moved to lean on the stage's edge
reached her ears and she ignored them. But she was
unable to ignore the hand that grasped her ankle. Her
quick move away was foiled by the surprising strength
of the grip. 'Foxy,' the boy leered up at her. He
couldn't have been more than seventeen, but she looked
around for one of the band anyway. But they were
eagerly reaching for their cigarettes and coffee at the
back of the stage.

'Let go please,' she said and made a sharp pull against his hold. Her grip on the guitar loosened and its weight slipped downwards cracking the boy's knuckles before she caught it further up on the neck. The youth snatched his hand away with a gasp and clapped the other one over his stinging fingers.

'Sorry,' Briony said. 'It's always dangerous to get too close to the stage.'

She turned her back and walked off. Jeff shook his head. 'Why didn't you just call me, love? You'd already mangled the poor kid's hands before I realised what was going on.'

'I didn't do it deliberately.' She bit her lips. 'It served him right though. I hate being mauled.'

'Don't I know it,' he said. 'Tell me if they bother you again.'

Duane watched her as she took some coffee from Colin, one of the road crew.

'A bit particular are you?' he sneered softly as he came to stand next to her.

She gave him a cool look but didn't answer.

'Now just what kind of a man would you consider suitable to handle a classy girl like yourself?' Duane went on. 'That one over there might be more your style. Trouble is, he looks as if he might think you're not good enough for him.'

Following his gaze she looked straight into the face that seemed to be haunting her tonight. 'A nice man' he certainly didn't look after all, and no accountant or bank manager she'd ever seen looked quite like him either. He strolled up to their group, glanced dispassionately around at them, then spoke to Jeff. Duane leaned forward until his cheek touched Briony's hair. He said softly, 'What about it then? Would his lordship be aiming high enough for you, milady?'

Jeff had a few words with the man then began to introduce him. 'This is one of the Gala organisers . . .' he began, but a deep voice interrupted.

'I want the volume reduced when you commence playing again. And I want your co-operation in avoiding any trouble with the crowd.' He paused and

Briony felt the cool eyes sweep over her. Blue eyes, she noticed in surprise—very blue, even in the poor lighting back here.

'Look, Mr—er . . . Barry. . . .' Jeff floundered over the name as usual and the man didn't offer to clarify it, just listened stonily. 'We don't look for trouble. In fact, we avoid it like the plague. We've got thousands tied up in our equipment and believe me, we like things nice and peaceable.' He grinned disarmingly but the tall man remained unmoved.

'The kind of retaliation I saw out front is not designed to keep the peace,' he said dryly.

'Oh that. Those kids were just a bit cheeky and Briony didn't mean to. . . .'

'She's offering plenty of provocation. The youths can't be blamed for thinking she's easy game.'

Briony opened her mouth to protest, her cheeks flaming with anger at the flat statement, but Jeff rushed in with the diplomacy born of his years of experience with hotel managers, club presidents and restauranteurs. He walked away with the man. Duane laughed at Briony's angry face.

'His lordship *definitely* doesn't think you're good enough for him,' he whispered.

All in all, Briony's smile was not so spontaneous when they resumed playing. The chocolate bar and coffee had not stopped the gnawing in her stomach and she felt the beginnings of a headache that began erratically but soon throbbed in perfect rhythm to the beat. She cursed herself for not eating properly that morning—or at lunch. Maybe if she had, the guitar wouldn't feel so heavy and maybe she wouldn't be so bothered by a dark face and flame-blue eyes. She sang the lead this time, roughening her voice and feeling the grate of it in her throat.

Song followed song and Briony began to be confused, though she continued to smile and react automatically to her cues. But an odd giddiness blurred her vision occasionally and she became light-headed. The heavy make-up was oppressive and she was damp with perspiration from the heat of the lights. One spotlight over her head burned down with all the tenacity of the summer sun.

The boys had disappeared from the front of the audience, Briony noticed. She wondered if the blue-eyed man had warned them off. It wasn't until the second to last number that she discovered just where they were.

The explosive sound of shattering glass came in the middle eight bars. Jeff pulled her back as a shower of hot glass fragments fell near her. Miraculously only a couple of shards caught in her hair and Jeff was still picking them out when another light exploded.

Dazed, Briony heard the crowd's voice swell in alarm, a few shouts and female shrieks punctuating the buzz as they fell back from the stage. The man Barry appeared briefly and shouted something to Jeff. Everything after that happened in a blur for Briony.

Ritchie who had been valiantly drumming on, leapt to his feet and began packing up his kit. The roadies, Mal and Colin, wheeled trolleys on to the stage and began moving the speakers and coiling up the power leads. Pushed to the rear of the dais by Jeff, Briony tried to brush the cotton wool from her mind and vision, but there was a soft hushing sound in her head and she looked about in vain for the cause of it. She heard Mike's voice, suddenly urgent as he grabbed Jeff's arm.

'It's those kids—they knocked out the lights with stones.'

'Yes I know, let's go.'

'But Duane's gone after them.'

Jeff groaned. 'Oh no. You load the blue wagon, Mike. I'll go get him, the damned fool.' As he went he shouted back to Mal, 'And get the amplifier out of the way fast—I don't want anything to happen to that.'

As the equipment disappeared, Briony hovered ineffectually, her efforts to help firmly dismissed by the road crew who were moving like greased lightning.

'Get in Jeff's car, Briony—I'm moving this one towards the gate.' Mike called to her as he and Ritchie drove away and the road crew moved off in the third vehicle. Briony waited a moment longer then moved around to the side of the stage to see if Jeff was all right. With relief she saw him coming back with Duane, who was rubbing the knuckles of one hand and looking very pleased with himself. They passed around the far side of the stage from her and she hastened to join them in the car. Before she could break from the shadowed back of the platform, a hand grabbed her shoulder from behind and she heard a guffaw of laughter.

It was the boy whose hand she had bruised earlier. He held her just long enough for Jeff to drive the station wagon away. Her shouts went unheard and she stared at the twin ruby lights of the car in disbelief.

'Serves you right,' the boy sneered in her ear as he released her. 'Better start walking, darling.' His friends joined him and they scuffed away in the darkness. The sound of motorcycles came moments later.

Briony didn't know whether to laugh or cry. Jeff had gone without her. But then, she had been spared worse by the youths who thought nothing of throwing rocks about with such disastrous results.

It was all a bad dream, she told herself, sagging against the stage decking. 'Quiet, restful surroundings. . . .' She almost giggled. Just fifteen miles away, Mrs Gordon had a nice little caravan and quiet, restful surroundings. She closed her eyes and could almost smell the new-mown grass and roses. She would wake up and find herself in Stocklea, a tidy sum of money in her pocket from the night's work with the band and no recollection of this crazy finale to the performance.

'When you make trouble you really do a thorough job of it.'

It *was* a bad dream. Briony kept her eyes shut at the steely tone of the voice. She knew just what face went with that voice—a severe, dark face with unexpectedly flame-blue eyes. She raised her lids and confirmed it. The disapproval she had sensed before was etched into his features now, making his eyes like flint, his mouth a harsh line. This was the last straw. To be hauled over the coals by him when what she really needed was to be comforted and held by someone. But the broad shoulders and strong arms of this man were not offering comfort. In fact, he looked quite capable of hitting her at this moment.

Briony took a step back and tried to think of something to say to him. But the hushing sound, like a gentle ocean swell, was louder now and she gazed at him wordlessly.

'I suppose you and your friends expect payment for this night's work? Have you any idea of the damage you've done? The spotlights were hired and will have to be replaced—half the crowd have gone home disgusted——' She lifted her chin a little higher, wondering why he was swaying. 'I should have never agreed to hire a group,' he said angrily, 'They're nothing but trouble.' He seemed to be waiting for some response but still she could find no words.

Shaking, she looked beyond him to the dark driveway, hoping to see Jeff coming back for her. How long, she wondered, before he found out she was not with any of the others?

'Your boyfriends have gone,' he told her with, she thought, a certain amount of grim satisfaction and she shook her head.

'Yes they have. I told them to go to avoid any further disruption. Though I did think they would collect their decorative singer.' He paused. 'I daresay you'll soon attach yourself to another group of undesirables.'

He took her arm and turned her towards the remaining light. Her face was white and strained, the hollows under her eyes accentuated purple against the pallor, the theatrical, glitter eyeshadow suddenly forlorn. She shook her head again and started to say—wanted to say—'They're not undesirables——' but the gentle ocean swell in her head turned into the turbulent roar of surf. 'Darn it,' she thought as the man's face slid upwards, 'I didn't bring a towel.'

Briony closed her eyes and slipped from his hold. He stood there frowning down at the slim figure of the girl crumpled at his feet. With a sardonic smile he bent over her, expecting to see the telltale quiver of the eyelids as she faked the faint. But her heavily mascara'd lashes remained still and his face grew grave as he noticed the ashen colour of her skin under the zany make-up. Quickly he gathered her up, surprised at the lightweight burden she made, and strode around the outskirts of the fair to the house.

Briony's lids flickered and she hazily tried to remember what she had been about to say. Something about a towel and the boys. . . . Her eyes flew open to alien surroundings. The ceiling was high and pearly grey in the muted light. Turning her head slightly she saw hundreds of books and the soft-shadowed edge of velour curtains. Baffled, she closed her eyes again and next time she opened them a man's dark head was outlined against the ceiling. Memory came creeping back and she struggled to sit up.

The hide upholstery of the couch beneath her was cold, so she assumed she had been there only a few minutes. Had she passed out? She couldn't recall anything beyond the man's scathing words to her near the stage. She reeled as she raised her head and the man's jacket sleeve was rough on her skin as he slipped an arm about her in support.

'Drink this,' he commanded, and she turned her head from the smell of brandy.

'Come on,' he prompted, 'I imagine you've sampled a lot worse than this.'

Heavens, he really did have a poor opinion of her. Now he had decided she was a hard drinker as well as all the rest. Weakly she gave up the struggle and sipped the drink as he held it to her lips. She was no match for him even when she was fit she guessed and right now she could put up no more resistance than a kitten. The brandy burned its way to her empty stomach. She really would be drunk unless she ate something soon to combat the brandy—then Mr Barry Whats-his-name would be convinced of her lack of character.

He looked down, unnervingly close with his arm still around her, and Briony abruptly registered the very positive feel of his hand on her bare shoulder and the pleasant tang of after shave or soap that lingered about him. But there was nothing positive or pleasant about his face. His eyes bored into hers from a disconcerting few inches and there was no Good Samaritan kindness in them. Letting her go he stood up and put the brandy glass down. 'Stay here and rest. I have to attend to a few matters outside. I'll be back and we'll see what's to be done with you.'

The door clicked curtly behind him and Briony levered herself from his couch. It was the kind she had only seen in film scenes set in exclusive men's clubs. Substantial, expensive and very masculine as was the rest of the room. '. . . we'll see what's to be done with you,' she muttered under her breath. She stood up, determined not to be here when he returned to dispose of her in whatever way he thought suitable. Briony scowled, then grimaced at a new bout of dizziness.

She sat down again and the faintness passed, leaving her reluctantly tied to the chesterfield. Although she wanted to get away, she had no wish to be found out cold by the man on his rich patterned carpet. Impatiently she waited to gain her strength, looking about at the room's solid warmth. The bookshelves were polished mahogany with tailored glass doors that threw back the gleam of the brass lamp to Briony. Sitting on the edge of the setted she glimpsed the reflection of her pale face and the cloud of hair that was even more tousled now. Wryly, she wondered if Mr Barry Whatever had had such an unconventional guest in his den before.

Briony stared at the desk and had no doubt that this was his den and his house. She could just imagine him sitting in that massive leather chair, working at the desk that bore the patina of a hundred years. On its antique surface was a collection of silver accessories—several pens and an old-fashioned inkstand and fittings, all silver, a paperweight and a superb, ornate cigarette box with a modern lighter. That little lot, she thought, casting an assessing eye over them, were probably worth more than the ill-fated car she was still paying off. With a sigh she stood up, moving experimentally until she was certain she would not collapse in an untidy heap in this inner sanctum. Curiously she looked over the book titles displayed behind glass. Architectural texts stood snugly alongside bound classics and staid-looking books on management and psychology. Lower down were paperbacks including an unlikely one called *The Skydiver's Book* and an even more unlikely copy of *The Goon Scripts*. Lower still were some modestly massed trophies. Briony leaned closer to see the name engraved on them. But all she could make out was 'Cricket Cap – –' on one and what looked like '– – crosse' on another. Lacrosse? Maybe some other fun-loving person lived here too—a lacrosse player with Goonish humour, she smiled and turned away past the desk, her hand trailing on the dark surface. She didn't know what the timber was, but it was dark and sympathetic to the Victorian design. Like the trolley near it, she thought, making cautiously for the door. Of the same deep-toned timber, it bore a tea tray and service that looked a gracious part of the last century. Her eyes moved on, flicked back quickly to focus on the tray. Beside the teapot and bone china cups was a plate bearing two rather small sandwiches on a linen napkin. A little dry and beginning to curl at the edges, they were surrounded by the crumbs of others long consumed. To Briony they looked delicious.

Her stomach, protesting at the meagre mix of chocolate and coffee and now brandy, gave an involuntary heave but her hand, outstretched to take the leftovers, hesitated. There was something demeaning, she decided, in taking the leavings of that disapproving man. She looked around the room again and felt like some street urchin in Victorian London, stealing food from a gentleman's parlour.

'Darn it. He'll never know,' she said aloud and picked up one of the sandwiches. 'Thanks, your lordship.' She mocked a curtsey. Just for a moment longer she savoured the anticipation then bit into dry but glorious ham and tomato. But one bite was all that she had before the door knob rattled. With a guilt that was out of all proportion, Briony swallowed and leapt away from the trolley, thrusting the unfinished sandwich behind her.

This was ridiculous, she thought. She should simply say, 'I hope you don't mind if I finish off these sandwiches.' If it was someone else, she might—but to admit her hunger to the man who stood at the door regarding her as if she was an escapee from Reform School would smack of degradation.

A mild hysteria almost made her giggle. What crazy twists of fate had brought her, garbed like some comic strip heroine or a Buck Rogers' extra, into this atmosphere of privilege and tradition? It was no wonder he looked at her as if she was a suspicious character. Briony backed away as he came into the room, knowing that she looked as guilty as if she had stolen one of his silver teaspoons, instead of merely helping herself to a crust. For the second time that night she searched for something to say to him but as she opened her mouth the man moved forward and grasped her arms none too gently. His head turned and he briefly looked at the collection of silver items on the big desk.

'All right. Let's see what you've got there.'

This was the moment to produce the sandwich, but Briony resisted the humiliation, dragging her wrist down as he closed a hand about it. With one arm he held her tight about the waist, his fingers against the bare skin below the sequinned top. With the other he applied a relentless pressure until her tightly closed fist was imprisoned where he could see it.

'Come on, Wonder Woman,' he said harshly and began to prise her fingers open. 'What have you taken? That was a very convincing trick to get inside the house—I suppose your friends are waiting to. . . .'

His voice stopped abruptly as he stared un-comprehending at the squashed remains of a ham and tomato sandwich. It was, Briony saw, almost entirely unrecognisable. Into the silence of the room drifted the strains of the carousel and the distant sound of voices. Held there, her wrist in his grasp, Briony's sense of the ridiculous grappled with a growing need to cry. A scene from an old movie flicked on in her head—Oliver Twist holding up his bowl and asking for more . . . she saw herself as one of the Bisto Kids, nose twitching with hunger and knew that this story would make amusing telling to Jeff one day. But there was nothing amusing about it now—nothing amusing at all. She was determined not to cry though. Not that. With this man watching in this beautiful, silent room.

'Sorry, sir,' she said at last in her best cringing Cockney, 'I stole a sandwich, sir.'

CHAPTER TWO

His fingers tightened about her wrist. 'Why the devil didn't you say what it was?' he bit out, then picked the crushed contents from her palm and tossed them on to the tray.

'I—I——,' Briony swayed and his arm went about her waist, his sleeve rough and warm against her bare skin. 'I felt guilty,' she said looking up again into those intense blue eyes. They were narrowed on her, searching her face and Briony felt dizzy again. The sensation of falling made her clutch at him, one hand finding the texture of his jacket, the other sliding beneath to the smooth, silken shirt fabric over his ribs. She withdrew her hand as from a flame and held on to the lesser intimacy of his jacket.

'What happened to the London accent?' he enquired.

'It—was a joke,' she said lamely, conscious of the entirely unhumorous sensation of being held in his arms, however impersonal and supportive they might be.

He gave a crack of laughter. 'A joke! I'm amazed that you can find anything to joke about tonight.' His tone was dry and as disapproving as ever, thinking of the spotlights no doubt, but he showed no inclination to let her go. Briony closed her eyes for a moment, wondering where her composure had gone. It must be the result of her first faint ever that made her wish she could put her head against his very capable shoulder and feel the security of his strength. . . .

'Put this on,' he said and released her to remove his jacket. 'You seem to make it a practice to borrow men's coats.' Through the cloth his hands were firm on her shoulders. He guided her to the chesterfield and pushed her down on to it. 'Don't move. I'll be back.'

He took the tray and went, leaving Briony dazed and obedient on the settee. Her hand went to the lapels of

his jacket drawing it closer around her. The mingled
smell of fabric and clinging after shave was potent, as if
the man was still in the room, holding her. Barry
Something ... she mused. The name didn't suit him
somehow. Her eyelids drooped and she let her head tilt
back against the supple leather. Jeff might have
discovered by now that she was not with them. She
should go and wait for him near the gate ... in a
minute, Briony told herself, she would do just that. ...

The sound of clinking china and more particularly
the smell of beef soup brought her bolt upright on the
couch. She watched in bewilderment as the man came
in and placed a tray on the table. Her stomach growled
but she felt like curling up in humiliation. Now she
really did feel like a poor little waif about to receive
charity.

He sat down opposite her in a single armchair and
took a bowl and spoon from the tray. Briony dragged
her eyes from him and saw that there were two servings
of soup and chunks of crusty bread, not just one.

'Eat before you pass out again,' he said shortly and
turned his attention to eating.

Had he guessed that she would hate to sit, a
supplicant, eating his charity while he watched? The
man showed a sensitivity that was almost her undoing.
But the delicious smell of the soup drifted up to her and
before she started looking like a Bisto Kid, she applied
herself to it. As she finished the curious meal, he rose
abruptly to his feet and Briony started so that her
spoon clattered in her dish. 'Don't worry,' he said
curtly. 'I won't eat you.'

It was the sort of assurance he might have given a
child and in the circumstances almost amusing. Did he
think she was afraid of him?

'No. But if it hadn't been for the soup it might have
been the other way around,' she smiled, warmed by the
food to some semblance of confidence.

His harsh mouth quirked and he paced away only to
turn and survey her. The sounds of the fair were far
away. In undeterred waltz time the carousel churned
out its music as if the distressing events of the night

might be erased by its ceaseless gaiety. Briony recalled that the house was some distance from it and the stalls. He must have carried her all the way here. She was disturbed by the thought.

Inside, the quiet was a capsule surrounding them both as their eyes held. He was faintly smiling as he shifted his gaze. 'I think even you might find me too tough to break a fast on Briony.'

'Even you'—there was a wealth of assumption in the words. Not that it mattered she thought, what this stranger believed of her.

'You know my name?'

'One of the—er—musicians called you Briony.'

The deliberate hesitation annoyed her. 'They are musicians you know, and good ones.'

'I'll take your word for it. But I suspect you're prejudiced. You seem on very—friendly terms with them all. Especially the leader.'

'Well yes, but that's because he's my——' 'brother' she was going to say when he cut in dryly.

'So I gathered. And what of the others? The affectionate Blackbeard and el Diablo who smoulders at you?'

He seemed to be implying that she was on intimate terms with them all and Briony resented it. At the same time she registered the fact that he had taken a keen interest in them. He had even noticed Duane's unwelcome attentions although, of course, he didn't believe they were unwelcome.

'Look, Mr——' she began but he sat down at the opposite end of the chesterfield and interrupted yet again.

'Never mind. It's really none of my business what your private arrangements are.'

He might be surprised to know just how dull—almost antiquarian—her private arrangements were, she thought. If of course he could believe them consistent with a girl wearing boots and a skimpy costume. Her gratitude was fast sinking under his interrogative manner. 'No. It is none of your business,' she said shortly.

He turned on the couch, twisting his body towards her as he crossed one elegantly clad knee over the other. In his expensive, tailor-made clothes he was tradition and substance Briony saw—as opposed to her own crazy appearance that epitomised the transience and glitter of another world. Not hers anymore—but he obviously thought so.

'Where are your parents? It should be their business to see that you're not running about with a group of scruffy boys, drinking no doubt and maybe worse and not eating properly. How often do you pass out as you did tonight?'

Briony looked back at him and could have said that she didn't do any of those things—that she and Jeff had been looking after themselves for a long time now. That a father who'd walked out on them while they were still at school and a mother who'd since remarried had not concerned themselves with them overmuch while they were under age and certainly didn't bother now. She could have said, too, that she longed to find a place for herself—that now and then it would be nice to lean on someone, but she closed her eyes tiredly and dropped her head back.

'How old are you?' his voice was harsh again suddenly.

'Twenty-two,' she told him and opened her eyes to look along the settee's length at him. She pulled his jacket closer around her and the tang of expensive cloth and after shave strengthened.

'You look younger,' he said at last and the roughness was gone from his tone.

'Is that why you kept frowning at me—because I looked too young to be playing in a band?'

His eyes wandered over her again and she was acutely conscious of the odd picture she must make, with his coat around her and her legs uncovered save for nylon tights and boots.

'Was I frowning at you?'

She stared. 'Of course you were. Unless the expression is habitual.' That might be true, she thought—the frown line was deeply marked in his forehead—laugh lines were noticeably absent.

'You could be right.' He put a hand to his brow. The gesture and the faint rueful smile that accompanied it made him suddenly more vulnerable than his hard features suggested. Briony had an overwhelming wish to know why he was such an odd mixture of arrogance and niceness. Niceness? The word didn't sit well on him as a description. Sensitive then, she thought, remembering those two plates of soup instead of a beggarly one. Her eyes lingered on the beautiful shape of his hands—strong, capable hands that looked as if they only had to carry out the bidding of a capable, clever mind. What did he do, she wondered—besides working for charity? An arrogant, sensitive man with tension written all over him and a kind of magnetism that made a mock of his ultra-civilised exterior? She longed to ask questions and realised with a shock that this stranger had her intrigued.

But she wouldn't ask him anything—or tell him anything either she decided in something akin to panic. There were enough imponderables in her life without adding another. Briony met his gaze and tore from it, shaken by her own intense interest in the man. She must be a little crazed tonight.

'Where do you live, Briony?'

His question dropped into the silence and lay there for a moment or two.

'Sydney,' she said in her new found caution. It could do no harm to admit that much. Sydney housed millions in anonymity.

'It's a big place,' he replied dryly. 'Whereabouts in Sydney?'

'Nowhere you'd know. Anyway—I—move about a bit.' She astonished herself by the lie. Why on earth did she feel threatened by his questions? It wasn't as if a man like this one would want to look her up.

'Ah. Depending I suppose on who you're—sharing accommodation with?' The thin lips curled in distaste again. 'Isn't that the way you young rebels do things?'

It was tempting to correct his supposition but she looked away with a shrug that could have meant anything. 'Sure, one place is as good as another,' she said, falling in with his expectations of her. If she had some gum, she could chew while she talked and complete the tough image. The punk rocker in the gentleman's parlour? Maybe Jeff could get a song from it.

'How long have you been travelling about with bands?' It wasn't an enquiry as much as an accusation. She could almost see the vivid scenes of depravity running through his mind. Why did everyone imagine that you had to be some kind of moral drop-out to perform with a band? 'Since I was fourteen I suppose.' Unconsciously she slipped into Cheryl's mode of speech and to finish it off she shrugged—a wonderful enigmatic Cheryl-type shrug. The man frowned and looked more closely at her. 'What were your parents thinking of?'

'What parents?' She felt a pang as she said it. That sounded as if they were dead, but somehow the fact that they were alive and uncaring made the question as valid. And sadder. A letter a year on her birthday and a card at Christmas—that was her parents. Briony's apprehension returned. Sitting here, communicating with this man could only lead to trouble ... 'trouble always comes in threes' the resigned tone of her mother's voice echoed in her ears.

'What is it about you that doesn't ring true?' he murmured and his narrowed gaze made her pull at the jacket again as if it was some sort of security. So he had noticed her change of manner. Briony made a moué of disinterest à-la-Cheryl and wished she'd never started this stupid imitation. It wasn't as if she'd ever see him again, so it couldn't really matter, but already she was regretting that she would leave behind a cheap, cheeky image. She looked up at him. He was still staring. How blue his eyes were. A tingling raced down her spine. Damn. Why couldn't he have been fat and fatherly? She had a clear conviction that she wouldn't be able to put this chance meeting from her mind for a long time.

'I have to go.' She got to her feet and hesitated as he did the same, blocking her passage.

'Where will you go?' The deep voice held her on the

spot, filled her with confusion. But she stuck her chin in the air like the tough kid he thought she was.

'My—Jeff will be back for me. I'll wait by the gates for him.'

'You could stand there for hours. And maybe encounter those louts again.'

'I can look after myself.'

He gave a grunt of disbelief. 'You may think you can Briony, but there are some situations you'd be better to avoid.'

She was wishing she could avoid this one. Edging sideways, she eyed the door behind him. 'Like what?'

'Like letting yourself get involved with people like that guitarist—the one in black. Like drifting about with no goals, no positive basis for your life. For God's sake get a job, settle down and meet some ordinary, decent people. . . .'

The sheer arrogance of it distracted her from the door. 'I know another situation I'll avoid like the plague in future,' she told him angrily, 'And that's getting stuck in the same room with an arrogant, prejudiced snob who wouldn't know the first thing about "ordinary people". Apart possibly from the one in black, the band are decent people, extraordinarily talented people and warm people, even if they don't come from your exalted socio-economic level.'

Now there was speculation mixed with anger in those spearing blue eyes and Briony guessed why. She had thrown her 'Cheryl' pose out the window with that little speech.

'So there's a brain under that bird's nest,' he said, 'And a good deal of resentment as well.'

What had she done now? The man was probably thinking she was an anarchist or radical. It was all too much. The events of the evening were catching up on her—Jeff might come back and miss her. Then what would she do? She bolted to the door, shedding all pretence. To get away was suddenly imperative.

But not possible. He caught her as she passed him and her breath escaped in a startled gasp. Her eyes were wide with dismay as his fingers burned the skin of her wrist. A stranger, she thought wildly—chance-met once and never again. What quirk of fate made her react to him as to no other?

'Let me go——' she said urgently. 'They might miss me at the gate.'

'They might have already missed you,' he pointed out and his eyes searched her face with intensity. As if he was looking for a piece of a puzzle. 'What will you do then, Briony? Take a lift with a stranger?'

'No,' she shook her head and her hair clouded across her face, 'I don't know—let me go——'

He caught a handful of her hair, tugged on it to make her face him. 'You can stay here tonight,' he said softly. A tiny warmth grew in those cool blue eyes and Briony watched it, her will diminishing. Abruptly her heartbeat changed tempo. It sounded like frantic bongo drums a trivial part of her mind noted while she gazed at him. 'No.' Her eyes slid away, looking at the lamp's soft glow where it sheened the upper folds of the velvet curtains, at the deep purple shadows where the light did not reach. She looked at the books behind their glass and down at the carpet. Anywhere but at him. Inevitably though, she had to.

The hawkish look was back on his face, enhanced by the shadow of the strong nose cast to one side, the angular lines of chin and jaw. His dark hair gleamed almost black making the light blue eyes burn more surprisingly in the bronze tone of his skin. He seemed angry—his jaw clenched tight so that the muscular effort rippled in his cheek.

'I must be crazy,' he muttered and his hand bunched the hair in his grasp, curved to the shape of her head. If he was crazy so was she. 'Move' she urged silently—'run'. But Briony stayed transfixed. The dark, compelling face and flame-blue eyes filled the screen of her mind and she knew that this stranger was going to kiss her and she wasn't going to stop him.

But the sound of voices outside penetrated the door and the veil that hung over Briony's consciousness. The man's sudden searing look of contempt brought her sickly back to earth. As the door began to open and he turned to it, she cast around for an escape route and finding none, sank into the corner of the chesterfield and curled up there in the shadow, wishing herself invisible.

A tall woman entered, followed by a much younger man carrying two parcels. With them came the incomparable smell of fried onions and meat. And even though food was the last thing on her mind now, Briony's stomach turned over at the aroma.

'Two hamburgers as you ordered, darling,' the low voice of the woman was amused and a little curious, but Briony caught the proprietary note there. The tall blonde was dressed to match the host, in elegant, carelessly expensive clothes and accessories.

'They've cleared away most of the glass and everything's almost back to normal but I'm afraid that vulgar scene has cost us some profit. A lot of people went home as soon as those louts started throwing rocks.'

They discussed the evening's events for a few minutes as the host went to a cabinet and poured drinks for them. His easy smile to the blonde struck a chord of anger in Briony. Laughable, to imagine that he had been about to kiss her. More likely he had been about to deliver another homily on her lifestyle. 'You can stay tonight'—that offer was probably a charitable one—on a par with a soup for the poor, fainting minstrel. Maybe she had let that half glass of brandy and the ambience of this mellow room deceive her into thinking that she'd seen desire in those cool eyes. Self-deception—she questioned herself—or wishful thinking? Or truth? As if it mattered. Briony glowered at the three beautiful people laughing at some more positive feature of the Gala. She had imagined the entire thing—dazed in her weakened state, and irritable she dragged his jacket close and wondered if she could make good her escape while they were all busy being pals.

But the small movement caught the eye of the tall woman. Her long fingers settled on the man's arm and she said, in a husky, blonde voice, 'But darling—what have you got there?'

For all the world, Briony thought sourly, as if she was a lapdog or a new ashtray. The younger man strolled closer, surveying her costumed figure with interest. His low wolf-whistle brought a frown to the faces of the other two. The dark man took the burgers from the desk where the younger had tossed them, and threw one to Briony. 'There you are. I ordered those while the soup was heating.'

She almost drooled at the powerful, beautiful smell of the food but hesitated to unwrap it. With a rustle of tissue the man sat down next to her and bit hugely into his hamburger. 'Mmm, not bad,' he looked sideways at her, oblivious apparently to the growing speculation in the eyes of his friends. 'Eat,' he said firmly. And Briony ate. Between mouthfuls, her host introduced her simply as 'Briony' to Neil Harvey and Elizabeth Campbell.

Elizabeth raised an eyebrow and said, 'Yes, I saw her with that dreadful band.'

Except that her mouth was full, Briony would have defended Silverhero. She swallowed hastily but Elizabeth had resumed.

'Why didn't she leave with the rest of them? Does she know Stuart?'

Stuart? Briony flicked a glance at the man. Who was Stuart? 'No,' he answered dryly, 'not as far as I know.'

Elizabeth's pale eyes licked over Briony, as fast and sharp as the tip of a whip, taking in the booted legs and crinkled hair. Her lips tightened a fraction as she recognised the jacket covering her bare shoulders. Briony simmered as they talked about her as if she wasn't there. 'What, darling, is she doing here?' the blonde repeated.

'She passed out,' Briony said clearly and the man's mouth twitched in amusement. The boy laughed. Elizabeth's finely moulded nostrils quivered and her mouth was a beautiful, compressed, straight line.

'Briony's friends seem to have been rather confused and left without her.' The odd blue eyes dwelt on Briony thoughtfully. 'I haven't found out yet where you want to go.'

'Does it matter?' Elizabeth was obviously suggesting

that he had done his duty. Briony was almost tempted
to mention that he had offered her a bed for the night.
But whose?

'Jeff will come back for me,' she said confidently,
hoping it would be soon. She didn't want to wait
around too long dressed as she was—it seemed to give
people the wrong idea. One thing was for sure, she
wouldn't tell these three where she was heading.
Stocklea was only a matter of fifteen miles away and
there was no guarantee that they weren't acquainted
with Mrs Gordon or someone who knew her. A quiet
word about tonight's fiasco would be no recommenda-
tion to an old lady seeking a conscientious gardener.

Briony stirred uneasily, lost in her thoughts. If she
got the job—her fingers crossed—Stocklea was a little
too close to this place for comfort. Her eyes went to the
man again. What she really meant was too close to him.
Still, she reassured herself, in the unlikely circumstance
that she was hired and ran into him again, he'd hardly
recognise her without the crinkles and the glitter.

Elizabeth's voice penetrated her abstraction.

'Ungrateful little wretch, isn't she?' the words were
addressed to the dark-haired man, but aimed at Briony
along with her equally cool gaze. 'You might at least
say thank you for being fed and looked after.'

The words were so Victorian that Briony almost
expected her to add, 'and stand up when you're spoken
to by your betters'. The woman must think her about
sixteen and negligible. Her temper rose and she eyed
Elizabeth for a moment then turned to the man who
had 'fed and looked after her' and tugged at an
imaginery forelock.

'Yeah, ta guv'ner.' She assumed the mock hopeful
look of a beggar not for the first time tonight and
caught the man's amusement. His hard mouth parted
and showed a glimpse of white, but there was
conjecture in the look he gave her.

A snort of disgust came from Elizabeth and the boy
Neil chuckled. He moved closer and looked Briony over
with a faint insolence in his eyes. It was a look she'd
seen many times before and discouraged in her Rivals

days. 'If you need a place to stay for the night, I could
fix some——' he began, grinning, and was silenced by
an icy glare from Elizabeth. 'Just being hospitable,' he
murmured as a knock sounded on the study door.
When it opened a big, heavy-set man looked in.

'Can you spare a minute, Ford?' Seeing the others, he
nodded in their direction. 'Elizabeth, Neil.' He nodded
to Briony too, then looked taken aback as he
recognised her as a member of the band.

They all went out, except Neil who grinned again and
stayed to renew his offer but a moment later the dark
man came back and ushered him outside. Her last
glimpse of him left behind a puzzling image of warm-
cold blue eyes and a mouth from which the smile had
vanished.

Ford. His name must be Barry Ford. It didn't fit him
somehow. It was a pity she hadn't got away before
she'd learned it though. The name crystallised all the
various impressions of him into a single, sharp imprint.
Footsteps clacked outside on the mellow, old stone of
the terrace and Briony got up.

She fairly flew through the house past bathrooms and
bedrooms until she found the back door. Thankfully
she let herself out on to a long terrace that was hung
with plants and glassed in with wide, sliding doors.
Opening one she stepped outside. The Gala's glow
turned her in the direction of the driveway and she
began to run, then stopped. The jacket still swung from
her shoulders. Carefully she took it off and hung it over
the back of a garden chair. The night air was damp on
her skin and her fingers trailed almost regretfully across
the warm, rough fabric. She should have thanked him
properly. Once more, she smoothed the jacket then
abruptly whirled and moved away to be swallowed up
by the darkness.

The carousel was still playing 'The Loveliest Night of
the Year'.

Jeff was furious when his car skidded to a halt outside
the impressive gates of Abingdon. Briony got in
gratefully. She had been standing for fifteen minutes,

shivering in the chill July air and hoping that the estate's disturbing owner would not find her again.

'I've a good mind to just take the Sydney road and not drive you to Stocklea after all,' he fumed. 'The rest of the guys are waiting for me at a roadhouse and I'm damned if I can see why I should keep them hanging about just because you couldn't be bothered getting in the car on time.'

'Jeff—I'm sorry, but——'

'Hell, Briony—I had your bag and turned off at Stocklea and it was another fifteen minutes before I realised the others had gone straight on. I had to chase them up before I found out you weren't with us. What a prize fool I look—having to round up my little lost lamb. And none of this would have happened if you'd just walked away from that young idiot instead of banging a Fender down on his hand.'

'But I didn't do it on purpose—it just slipped——'

She felt miserable. Guilt assailed her that she had prompted the whole disaster and the oddest feelings of regret sat like a stone in her chest. The tears that she had repressed earlier sprang to her eyes and her voice wobbled.

'Yes—well——' Jeff's voice steadied from anger to uncertainty. 'Bry—are you alright?'

'Yes of course I'm alright,' she burst out, sniffing and dashing tears from her cheeks. 'I've had broken glass showered over me, seen my brother rush off to break up a fight, been mauled by those stupid boys again and—and fainted at the feet of the most arrogant, insulting man I've ever met. Why shouldn't I be alright?'

'Mauled? What do you mean?'

Briony took the handkerchief he passed her and dried her face. 'Well—perhaps "mauled" was a bit strong. At any rate those boys stopped me from reaching the car just as you were driving off.'

'Did they hurt you?'

She shook her head.

'Who was the arrogant, insulting guy?'

Briony thought of the brief glimpses of concern and sensitivity she'd had beneath the man's cool exterior.

'Maybe "arrogant and insulting" was an exaggeration,' she admitted with a sniff. 'He did catch me—I think.'

'Was it old—whatsisname—Barry?'

'His name's Barry Ford I think,' Briony said, much calmer now and sorry she'd mentioned him. 'Not that I imagine you'll remember the name. Where's my bag?'

'In the back. Sorry I blew my top, Bry. I was a bit worried about you actually.'

'So I gathered. Only worried parents and big brothers chew out their lost lambs when they find them again.' She scrambled over the back of her seat and pulled the bag on to her lap. 'Now just be an understanding big brother and keep your eyes on the road while I get out of this ridiculous outfit.'

Ten minutes later Cheryl's costume was neatly folded on the loaded back seat with the boots and Briony breathed a sigh of relief.

'How marvellous to wear jeans again. I'm not cut out to be Wonder Woman. . . .' Her voice trailed off as she remembered the man Ford calling her that, his deep voice harsh with anger. Had he gone back to the study yet to discover that his waif had gone? Would she worry about that, she wondered. Probably not. But he would count the silver. . . .

'He caught you, did he?' Jeff murmured. She looked quickly at him. 'When you fainted?'

'I'm—not sure. All I know is I woke up and he made me drink some brandy.'

'Do you think he fancies you?' he went on mildly. 'He was giving you the eye tonight.'

Briony laughed off the suggestion. 'You could stay here tonight' the man had said. 'Don't be silly, Jeff.' Her brother gave her a curious look but let the subject drop.

'Here it is. Stocklea Hotel.' Jeff said a few minutes later as he pulled in to the kerb outside a two-storied building with iron lace balconies and green shutters. It was after closing time for drinkers and the verandah tables were empty. Only a light over the foyer proclaimed its willingness to offer accommodation.

'Would you like me to come in with you?'

'Oh no,' she said quickly, and leaned across to kiss his cheek. 'I've held you up long enough. Thanks Jeff.'

'Are you sure you'll be okay? Mike reckons there are no trains through here on a Sunday—how will you get back after the interview?'

'I'll just stay here another night,' she said cheerfully and made an embracing gesture that included the hotel. 'Whatever happens I'll phone you tomorrow.'

For the second time that night she watched the red lights of Jeff's car retreat. When they had gone she ruefully eyed the hotel as she picked up her bag and set off along the street, thinking how very simple it was to burn your bridges. At the corner a signpost directed her to the Railway Station and as she passed rows of darkened houses hoped that there was a Saturday night train even if there wasn't a Sunday one. If not then her alternative accommodation for tonight was likely to be shut.

It was not. Inside the Stocklea Station Ladies' Room, Briony gazed around at the spatter-painted walls, lit by a single naked bulb for which there was no switch. 'Welcome to the Hilton, Madame. . . .' she muttered to her pale reflection in the mirror and attempted the cocky grin she felt should accompany her daring. Somehow it didn't come off and she went to the timber bench that ran along one wall and dropped on to it in sudden dejection. What on earth was she doing here in this dingy place, staying on for a dubious interview for a job she wasn't qualified to do?

The vinyl bag made a pillow of sorts and Briony stretched out on the hard bench and stared up at the beamed roof. 'Quiet, restful surroundings'—that was why she was here. She closed her eyes and conjured up visions of a neat caravan and roses—lots of roses. Her fingers crossed, then crossed a little harder as a man appeared in her rose garden. A man with a frown etched into his brow, but laughter waiting to be reached in his flame-blue eyes. . . .

She woke to the sounds of Sunday—a sleepy pastoral silence that smote her city ears like a new, deafening noise. Pale sunlight strayed through the small window high up in the wall and illuminated the unlovely interior. The light bulb that had been on last night was off now—apparently on an automatic circuit.

In spite of the discomfort she had slept soundly and hadn't heard a train come through last night, or this morning. Apparently no one had come in or she would have been marched off to the police station by now as a vagrant. She had half expected to be challenged when she'd come on to the platform last night. As she'd tiptoed past the Station Master's office the sensation of being watched had been overpowering. But the radio had been playing inside and nobody appeared to demand a ticket or a reason for her presence.

Optimism rose cautiously in her. At least the worst was over now. If she had to stay on tonight, she had enough money for a night in the hotel. As she rose and stretched her stiff limbs, she reflected that it was just as well. The Stocklea 'Hilton' was not the most comfortable lodgings.

The speckled mirror showed her a ghastly countenance. The glitter eyeshadow clung grittily in drifts beneath her brows and most of her make-up had retreated to her hairline, leaving her face pallid. And around it all, her hair sprang out in a dark, crimped mass. She set to work brushing water through it to straighten it again, then scrubbed her face clean with cold water and Jeff's handkerchief.

Briony's eyes were reddened and tearful before the glitter came off. 'Delicate,' she muttered to her image when she was free of the stage make-up. 'You look delicate my dear. I don't think you'll manage gardening.' She could almost hear the unknown Mrs Gordon say it. It was the worst she'd looked for months—just when she wanted to look hale and hearty enough to wield a shovel and spade in Mrs Gordon's garden.

But by the time she'd applied some light make-up and carefully blotted out the shadows under her eyes she looked better. The redness went away and she dried her hair on the sorry-looking handkerchief, then used her brush until the crinkles were gone. She swept her smoothed hair up into a conservative roll at the back and fancied that she looked quite respectable, even in her jeans. If only she looked stronger. Briony delved into her bag and found Jeff's plaid jacket which she'd forgotten to give back to him. Underneath it was a bulky jumper and she slipped it on hoping to disguise her slender figure. 'Not an amazon,' she told her reflection, 'but better.'

Ardently she wished for breakfast. Thank goodness she had eaten something last night she thought, and quickly banished the visions of soup and hamburgers shared with the disturbing Mr Ford. That was an episode, she insisted, ignoring the pang of regret . . . the enigmatic man would remain just that. An enigma. As for now, Briony zipped up her bag, all she would like to be intimately acquainted with was a shower and a cup of coffee, but neither would be forthcoming in the Stocklea Station Ladies' Room.

CHAPTER THREE

THE railway platform was bathed in sunlight. Large pot plants were scattered along its length and a small garden crammed with flowers glowed near the entrance. Briony took a careful look around and seeing no one decided on a confident, open walk to the street. Half way there she was stopped in her tracks by a voice.

'Sleep well?'

Guiltily Briony turned to confront the grey-haired man who was serenely watering a robust philodendron. He looked up and smiled.

'Don't worry love, I'm not about to turn you in. Saw you slip in there last night. Had a feeling you'd come for the night.'

'But aren't you supposed to report me?' Briony didn't like to suggest the possibility but was too curious not to ask.

'Oh yes, must report vandals and vagrants. Too right. But there, you're not one of those are you?' He lifted his chin to peer through bifocals at the leaves of the plant, examining them back and front.

She smiled, 'I haven't written on the walls or broken a window or anything.'

'Well, there you are,' he said comfortably and inspected her neat figure and smoothed-back hair. His gaze lingered on her face. 'Not a vandal—nothing like. Short of a dollar maybe?' he enquired and she flushed.

'Well, yes.' She found herself walking alongside him, stopping when he applied water to another plant, telling him who she was and about the job that kept eluding her in the city, the rising rental of her flat. Even about the untimely fate of the Volkswagen.

'So, I—er—got a lift to Stocklea and slept here to save money,' she finished up, deeming it wise to leave out all mention of Silverhero and the Gala fête just fifteen miles out of town.

'And Mrs Gordon's kindly agreed to interview me this morning . . .' she glanced at her watch dubiously. 'Of course it's very early, so perhaps——'

'Amy's an early riser. She'll have been up and about for hours already.'

'You know her? Could you tell me how to get to her house Mr—er?'

'George Olsen. Call me George. If you like to wait a few minutes I'll be locking up and I can walk you around there. I live a stone's throw from Sandalwood Street.' He emptied the can into a container of ferns and ambled off with a smile at her.

Briony waited for him by the bright flower garden at the station's entrance.

'Is this your work, George?' she asked, indicating the flowers when he came out. He nodded.

'Does—er—Mrs Gordon like this sort of garden?' she prodded, hoping that the old lady didn't have anything so ambitious.

'Roses and carnations,' he said and pulled closed the iron-barred gates of the station and locked them with a large Victorian-style key. 'Yes Amy's fond of her roses. . . .' George went on and took her bag from her under protest that she was perfectly strong and healthy enough to carry it for miles.

'Don't worry love. I'll give it back to you before Amy sees you.'

'You're a shrewd man, George,' she smiled at his accurate guess that she would not wish to arrive for her interview like some delicate female with a man carrying her bag. He quizzed her gently, drawing the extent of her experience from her in bits and pieces. It didn't take long.

'She'll want you to look after the pool, I expect,' George told her. 'The last one did. Mind you, he was a man.'

'Pool?' Briony stopped on the path. 'There was nothing about a pool in the ad and Mrs Gordon didn't mention it.'

'There's a pool all right,' George nodded. 'Amy swims a lot in summer.'

An uneasy fluttering began in Briony's stomach. This was more difficult than she thought. She'd imagined her biggest stumbling block to be her sex, but now other obstacles were appearing. Roses and carnations she just might be able to contend with—but a pool! Somehow she had an image of a frail little old lady in an old, old house with too much garden to look after herself. The pool didn't seem to fit. Suddenly Jeff's 'oldie' was throwing aside her warm milk and swimming. Her optimism seeped away the closer they walked to 18 Sandalwood Street. Even George's kindness could rebound on her. He had only to say that she slept on the Railway Ladies' bench to make quite the wrong impression on Mrs Gordon.

'Here we are. And there's Amy in the front garden.' Briony saw a tiny figure bent over a garden bed, the face obscured by a large hat.

'Good luck my dear,' he handed her the bag.

'George, I don't know why you've been so kind but—I'm very grateful.'

'You're from the city,' he smiled. 'A bit of a blind eye and a helping hand is nothing special down here.'

'Thanks anyway.'

'Amy,' he called to the woman who was standing now, 'this is your new gardener.'

Which was, Briony felt, assuming a bit much.

Mrs Gordon came over to the fence, stripping off her pik-flowered gardening gloves. She seemed a little surprised and her bright eyes fixed disconcertingly on Briony for some moments before she glanced at George.

'Now don't you pre-empt me, George Olsen,' she said briskly, then smiled at Briony. 'Glad to meet you, my dear.'

George took a pipe from his pocket and stuck it in his mouth, patting his pockets as he went on, undismayed, 'We've had quite a chat about collar rot, haven't we Briony?'

He winked at her and she flushed as Mrs Gordon gave her a curious look.

'Oh—er——' she stammered, torn between amusement at George's blatant attempt to make her appear knowledgeable and embarrassment at misleading Mrs Gordon. Not, she thought, that that lady looked as if she could be easily misled.

'Don't you light that darned thing up, George.' Amy Gordon said as he found his tobacco.

'Come on, Amy. You never let me light up indoors but out here surely I can't offend that sensitive nose of yours.'

'Sensitive my eye,' the little woman responded. 'That tobacco of yours gives off an odour that could fell an ox.' The tobacco pouch went back into George's pocket and he spread his hands expressively at Briony.

'See how it is? The only woman I've ever known who doesn't like the smell of a pipe. Damned masculine smell that—mach—what's the modern word for it?'

'Macho,' Briony grinned.

'That's it. Macho.' George shook his head. 'How the devil can a man be macho when he's only allowed to chew on his pipe?'

'Go home, George, and be as macho as you like,' Amy Gordon told him. 'And don't forget our card game on Monday night.'

'Don't know why you always say that, Amy—I only forgot the once in twenty years.' George strolled off along the quiet street and Briony watched him disappear behind the street plantings of oleander.

The houses were spaced wide apart and Mrs Gordon's frontage was double that of the others. It was obvious why she needed someone to take care of her garden. The side fences extended a long way back behind the house, garden bordering every inch of the way and the front was divided into several neat beds of roses and carnations. The house was set well back—an early colonial with wide, wide verandahs and ornate iron lace balustrading along them and on the steps mounting to the front door. The doors and windows, protected by the generous overhang of the verandah were further shaded by an enormous fig tree which was established halfway between house and fence. It spread its venerable branches protectively over a host of staghorn, elkhorn ferns and tree orchids attached to its trunk. The house and maybe the tree must be at least sixty years old, Briony thought, and both had aged beautifully.

But it was the air that delighted her. Briony sniffed then took several deep breaths before she felt Mrs Gordon watching her.

'The air——' she explained sheepishly, 'It really does smell of roses.' Immediately she felt a fool as the woman's eyebrows rose. But Mrs Gordon smiled, removed her hat and led the way to the house.

'Come in, Miss Wilde. You're early but I'll make us some tea.'

She smoothed back silver hair from her face and turned to look at Briony's flushed face.

'Dear me, you must be warm in that thick sweater.' Her eyes, faded grey-blue were shrewd and penetrating. Briony was reminded of someone fleetingly but Mrs Gordon smiled and the familiarity disappeared. All the same, she felt the futility of trying to fool this woman. Perspiring under the bulky jumper even on this winter's day, she realised how naive she had been to think it would make her look husky and outdoor-sy. In fact at the rate she was perspiring, it was more likely that she would be even slimmer when she took it off.

Mrs Gordon left her in a sitting room which was packed with elegant pieces of antique furniture. Crocheted mats frothed under ornaments, vases, lamps. Briony was no expert but she guessed that a great many of the room's furnishings were very valuable. The walls were host for framed pictures and photographs, many hanging in the old-fashioned way from the picture rail that ran round the high-ceilinged room. Water colours and faded sepia photographs in oval frames clustered over a walnut pianola and its matching cabinet full of rolls.

Amy Gordon brought a tray into the room and set it down on an inlaid table. She chatted about the weather and general topics as she poured tea and offered small cakes and cracker biscuits. Briony had to stop herself from falling upon the dainty offerings. Ensconced in the bygone comfort of a vast armchair with great rolled arms plumply stuffed, Briony felt that she had stumbled on to the stage set of an English play, where the Vicar was about to make his entrance.

Smiling politely she took a cup and saucer from Mrs Gordon and managed to nibble restrainedly at a cake while her stomach roared for more.

'Now,' said Mrs Gordon as she settled back into her own armchair, 'why do you want this job?'

The business-like attitude, so close on the heels of the genteel tea ceremony was uncannily like the psychological interview methods beloved of television police. Briony abandoned her images of fluffy old ladies and decided on the direct approach. She had a feeling that nothing less would appeal to Mrs Gordon.

She told her why she wanted the job, without revealing her illogical yearnings for the quiet restful surroundings promised by the advertisement. The caravan was especially attractive she admitted, and steady work—and outdoors work at that. In return the old lady mentioned the salary and some of the duties.

'Gardening experience?' she enquired. Briony proferred the McPhersons' reference and Mrs Gordon read it.

'They seemed to be very fond of you,' was her comment and Briony's heart sank. Regardless of her gentle hints, dear old Mrs McPherson, whose eyes were the better equipped of the two, had insisted on writing things like 'a lovely, sweet girl' and 'considerate and a pleasure to have around' instead of concentrating on her lawn cutting and shrub trimming. But she had decided any reference that even mentioned gardens was better than none.

'And you cut the lawn for them and—er?' Mrs Gordon probed.

'Trimmed the shrubs. And weeded. And watered it, of course.' Lord, how very scientific she sounded. Briony thought of the crammed flower beds out the front, of the fernhouse glimpsed at one side, of the ferns and lilies trees and shrubs that coursed along Mrs Gordon's boundaries. Of course she wouldn't want someone looking after all that who couldn't claim anything more skilful than lawn-mowing.

'But I learn very fast,' she said suddenly, remembering the beguiling smell of late roses—the immense and wonderful silence of Sandalwood Street and unwilling to let it go without a fight. 'And most libraries have marvellous books on gardening.'

'Mmmm.' Two shrewd, considering grey eyes bored into Briony and she tried to think why they should remind her of someone. . . .

'Clearing the pool?'

Briony shook her head regretfully. 'But I could get a book——'

'—from the library?' the old lady smiled suddenly and the grey eyes danced with amusement. Hope rose again in Briony and she cast about for something—some skill she might have that would tip the scales in her favour. 'I can mend a fuse,' she offered, and Mrs Gordon chuckled.

'That could be very useful,' she admitted. 'But my dear, I couldn't help noticing. You don't look strong.'

'I normally do. It's just that lately I haven't been eating . . .' horrified at the admission, her voice petered out. Firmly she closed her mouth and raised her chin proudly to dispel any impression of self-pity.

'More tea, Briony?' the sweet little old lady was back again, lifting the teapot graciously. 'Of course as I told you I was really looking for a man for the job. You do drive I suppose?'

Briony nodded and thought wryly of the Volkswagen now on the scrap heap.

'I have a car but hate to drive you see. Harry used to drive me out and pick me up.' She sipped her tea. 'There are such a lot of jobs to be done and I wonder if you would be up to them all.'

The ormolu clock on the mantelpiece ticked loudly while Amy Gordon finished her tea and reflected. Finally she put down her cup and rose. 'Perhaps you should see the caravan and facilities, Briony. After all, you might decide they're not what you'd like after all.'

This was a polite way of letting her down, Briony decided and followed her through a polished hall into a sun room at the back of the house. It was full of old-fashioned cane furniture and plants growing in every

conceivable type of container. Blue Delft jars and
Wedgwood dishes grew delicate maidenhair ferns and
ceramic pots hung in macrame slings almost hidden by
fronds and shiny pothos leaves. On the floor stood
several large urns of Indian design out of which thrust
the stems of indoor palms. Happily singing in this
paradise was a yellow canary in a bamboo cage.

'Hello Victor,' Mrs Gordon said to the bird as they
went through.

The back doors opened on to a large flagged area
which stretched to the edge of a pool. More plants
clustered in pots on the paving and several statuettes
stood on the waters edge in worn classical elegance.
Beyond that was a low building which Mrs Gordon said
was dressing rooms and amenities.

'The caravan is behind the cabana,' she said as they
skirted the pool, 'so that whoever uses it can also use
the pool facilities. Power is connected through, of
course. And Stanford insisted on a buzzer in the van so
that I could signal Harry if necessary, but I've never
used it.' Harry, she explained was the previous live-in
gardener. She didn't say who Stanford was.

The caravan was medium sized with a stained timber
structure at the door to form an annexe. Behind it, the
bare branches of a Japanese maple rose, a few brilliant
leaves still flying—flags to a departed autumn. Briony
eyed its delicate form and sighed.

'Harry built some timber steps as you see, and there's
a garden bed already dug around the van. Have a look
inside.' Briony looked. Wistfully she viewed the
compact kitchen with its fold-away table and com-
prehensive fittings, even an oven—the double bed
tucked economically into one end and partially
screened—the fitted wardrobe and drawers. It was
impersonally neat and empty, but she could imagine her
guitar leaning against the narrow divan there, and her
books on the shelf beside the bed. . . .

'Of course, the family will be annoyed with me for
making a decision without consulting them. Especially
Stanford. He worries that I'll get—ah—"mugged",
that's the word.'

Briony hardly heard the words, but one phrase leapt out at her. 'Making a decision'. Slowly she turned and looked down from the top step.

'You'll want to start right away, I expect, Briony? If you still fancy the job of course.'

'You mean I can . . . I've got——?' Briony fairly flew down the caravan steps and before she could think about it, bent and kissed Mrs Gordon's cheek. 'Thank you.'

'Well, I daresay I'll be called an old fool. Just mind you don't let me down girl.' The old lady had drawn away from Briony's impulsiveness, not altogether displeased, but taken aback.

'There are enough tinned supplies in the cupboards to start you off and I'll give you milk and eggs when you fetch your bag from the house. And,' she ran her eye over Briony's slim figure undisguised by the big sweater. 'You look as if you could use some. You'll have to stay overnight now. There's no train until tomorrow.' The old lady's head nodded. 'Now, you can drive me to church.'

That night Briony lay blissfully between the clean sheets of the big bed. She had enjoyed a long, hot shower, eaten a large, hot lunch and explored her new territory with Mrs Gordon as guide. She made immediate use of her own private laundry and the sight of her slept-in jeans and T-shirt on the clothes line gave her a ridiculous satisfaction. With a light heart she had almost skipped along the route back to Stocklea's post office to phone Jeff.

'I suppose I should say congratulations,' Jeff said, 'But frankly, I think you'll be sorry.'

'No I won't. The caravan is super, Jeff. I can't wait to get my things and settle in.'

'A place of your own eh, Bry?' there was understanding at last in Jeff's voice.

'I guess that was why I wanted this job so badly. Somehow I had a good feeling about it right from the start.'

Jeff asked a few more questions and finally chuckled. 'All right then. Congratulations.'

'Thanks. I think it was the McPhersons' reference and my own modest admission that I could mend fuses that won me the position.'

He laughed again. 'Are you sure Mrs Whatsit's not a bit gaga?'

'Mrs *Gordon* is a shrewd and discriminating employer,' she told him loftily, and he snorted.

'I believe you, thousands wouldn't. By the way—our friend from the Gala fête rang me to say that we'll get our cheque this week.

Briony's heart began its bongo rhythm again. 'Our friend?'

'The one who was arrogant and insulting—was that before or after you fainted?'

'Never mind—what did he say? And I don't mean about the cheque.'

'How do you know there's something else?'

'Woman's intuition,' she said striving for light-heartedness while the drums beat.

'Ha! Well—he wanted to know where you were.'

'What did you tell him?' she heard the abnormal pitch of her voice too late.

'I was a bit vague—I don't think he knows I'm your brother somehow.' After a pause he added, 'Are you sure he was insulting?'

'Yes—no. It doesn't matter. Jeff—I'll see you when I come back tomorrow. I have to say goodbye to a few people and tell the Rocco's I can't play for them anymore.'

'Okay, Bry. Be seeing you honey.'

The clean sheets crackled a little as she drew them up to her chin. Her eyelids drooped and a beatific smile curved her mouth. How she looked forward to filling the cupboards with her things, hanging up her one painting—sitting on the steps playing her guitar. And she would have some spare money from last night to buy in a few things.

It was something of a bonus to be paid after all. Briony had written off last night as a painful experience. 'He wanted to know where you were' Jeff had said. Her eyes flew open again. Why did he want to

know? And if he found out, would he look for her?
Scowling, she drew the bedclothes up to her ears. Too
much imagination, that had always been her trouble . . .
and too vivid a sense of recall. His severe bronze face
with those startling blue eyes presented itself readily in
her mind. She turned over, saw a few stars through the
skylight window and sighed. That was yesterday. The
confusing Mr Ford had no place in her new life.

Within three days Briony had found home. She
returned to Sydney and tied up all the loose ends of her
life there. Strangely, and sadly, there were less than she
expected. The city let her go with regrets from a few
friends and the Rocco's who showered her with Italian
emotion and assurances that if she ever wanted to come
back to sing they would welcome her.

Now her caravan was warmly hung about with her
belongings. Her one and only painting on a tiny patch
of wall, her books on a shelf. She sat, her first night
back, on the caravan steps and played her guitar and
sang in quiet contentment.

A small prayer plant stood on her table in its plastic
pot. She had purchased it at Stocklea and felt rather
ridiculous coming back with it to the house that was
festooned with exotic plants. When Mrs Gordon saw it
she scolded, 'For goodness sake girl, if you want plants
just say so. I've got hundreds.' Later she arrived at the
van with a copper bowl for the plant. Then she gave
Briony the keys of the storage locker in the cabana.
'There are two patio chairs in there and a table for your
annexe. For goodness sake don't start arguing. Get
them out and get that van looking like home.' Briony's
regard for the old lady grew quickly to affection. In her
brisk way she had taken her under her wing. In fact so
much so that Briony felt Mrs Gordon was preventing
her from handling the heavy work.

So far she hadn't done a lot to earn her pay.
Sweeping the flagstones and watering the garden.
Driving Mrs Gordon about in the five-year-old sedan to
visit friends or do her shopping. Cleaning the pool—
with the help of the manual. Of course there were a

couple of setbacks. The pool filter had its eccentricities which baffled her at first and a sortie into the shrubbery sent her out again with a wasp's welcome. But those aside, it was all too easy.

Suspiciously, remembering Mrs Gordon's frequent allusions to her 'skin and bone' figure, she asked the old lady if she was molly-coddling her and almost had her head snapped off.

'Just do what I ask, Briony. One day I'll have you running around so fast you won't know what hit you. As for now just prepare yourself.'

Briony clicked her heels together smartly and saluted. 'Yes, Ma'am,' she said in her West Point voice.

Amy Gordon's eyes twinkled appreciatively. 'You'd better be prepared to be looked over by my family too. I've managed to keep the arrival of my new gardener quiet to give you time to settle in but they'll be dropping in soon now to check you out.' She patted Briony's arm. 'Don't worry. I know exactly what they'll say—about you being a girl and such—so I'm ready for them.'

'It's natural that they'd worry,' Briony said, hoping that the family didn't take exception to her. 'It could be dangerous having someone living so close, I suppose.'

'Dangerous?' Amy Gordon hooted. 'That isn't what bothers my niece. What worries Margot is that someone might steal the valuables before she inherits them. Poor Mrs Pratt nearly had the vapours when Margot gave her a grilling.' Mrs Pratt cleaned the big house three times a week. She came and went by the front door and Briony had only seen her once, shaking her mop out the back.

Niece Margot, Briony discovered was not highly regarded by Amy Gordon, nor was her husband Doug. On the other hand, nephew Stanford could do no wrong. The bits and pieces she gleaned about him seemed to establish him as a middle-aged man who had once excelled at almost every sport there was, but who now only found time to 'come down and ride as reserve with the club' whatever that meant. Riding, tennis, golf—could Stanford ever have been as accomplished as

Mrs Gordon claimed? But whatever he had or had not been sportingwise, Stanford apparently was pretty much tied to his desk now and Briony pictured the former sportsman succumbing to flab and finance. According to his aunt he managed the family affairs with the same excellence that had marked his one-time sporting efforts.

After she met Margot Drewett, she came to the conclusion that Stanford wouldn't need to be anything special to be an improvement. The woman was fashionably thin and expensively groomed. Her eyes were slightly protuberant and a pale, pale blue. When she set them on Briony they were openly disapproving.

'But she's too young,' she cried to her aunt. 'What sort of a background does she come from? How can a girl handle the heavy work?'

All of that while Briony stood beside her, irked at being talked about as if she was invisible. It reminded her of that night in the tall man's study. And that reminded her of something else too—but she couldn't think what it was.

Doug Drewett was as unimpressed as his wife. Briony was conscious of having failed the inspection by two members of the family. But luckily it didn't matter as Amy Gordon took pleasure in running counter to their suggestions. The nephew could be another matter though. A good first impression on him was rather more important. And for some reason Briony was rather nervous about that.

But luck was with her. Mrs Gordon confided that Stanford was away on one of his business trips which gave her a couple of weeks to make her mark on number Eighteen Sandalwood Street before he came to look her over. As the days passed, Briony grew more confident. Though she never seemed to perform any arduous duties, Mrs Gordon was quite obviously satisfied with her. The old lady's social calendar was packed and Briony spent a good deal of time driving her to luncheons, committee meetings, bridge and to golf. Mrs Gordon couldn't get enough golf. She played several times during the week and every Saturday

afternoon. Not surprisingly she was very good, as
Briony found out when she arrived too early to collect
her employer from the course on her second Saturday
in residence at Stocklea.

The game was clearly far from over, so Briony skirted
Stocklea's magnificent course and made her way
through a thicket of shrubs and trees that clustered
around a creek. There was a narrow wooden bridge
across the water and Briony stood there a while,
dreamily propped on the splintering rail and watching
the small darting shapes in the creek. Two weeks since
she'd sung with the band—two weeks and everything
had swung around from chaos to contentment. If only
she could put that man out of her mind. The image of
him in that golden-toned room was clear—too clear to
dismiss. What if—she had conjectured a dozen times
since then—what if she'd met him some other way?
Would there have been that odd awareness between
them? It bothered her. Enough to make her sharply
observant whenever she took Mrs Gordon to the shops.
It was quite possible that they could bump into him—
possible even, she admitted, that Mrs Gordon knew
him. But she didn't ask, shying away from knowing.

On this fine, still day though, when the skies arched
overhead heartbreakingly blue, Briony shrugged off her
pestering doubts. The creek, which wound on through
the golf greens, marked the course's boundary at the
bridge and she crossed it and followed a winding path
to one of the large tracts of open land that abounded
around Stocklea. It was occupied by boys' cricket teams
and their supporters. Past them she could hear cheering,
and wandered around the perimeter of the cricket field
to see what lay beyond a staunch line of fig trees like
the one Amy had in her front garden.

She frowned as she saw the helmeted, booted riders
on their gleaming mounts. Polo? No. The players
wielded a sort of net on a stick. Polocrosse—that was it.
Curiously she leaned on the single rail fence. A small
tent was set up on one side of the ground, presumably
to provide teas and refreshment and further along was a
row of horse floats and vehicles. Briony shuffled,

uneasy for no real reason and watched the horses weaving and circling, the dust puffing about their banded legs, their sweat spraying finely from necks and haunches. It made a superb picture she thought, and straightened as the players veered towards this far side of the field. Few people stood here and Briony found out why as a great plume of dust from the grassless ground found her. There was another burst of cheering and a few whoops from the players as they milled around patting each other's backs. Through teary eyes Briony saw that the game had come to a finish. Dust coated her slacks and vest. She shook her hair and sneezed as more powder was released.

'Sorry about that,' one of the players called cheerfully, 'It wasn't me—it was the horse.'

She nodded and smiled. Another rider moved up beside the speaker and something about him froze Briony. His helmet was pulled low over his eyes—but that jaw—the set of those shoulders ... her hands feebly flicked the last particles from her sweater and vest, then she turned and walked away. It isn't him, she said firmly. Of course not. Why on earth did she get the urge to run? Her stride lengthened until she was in the dense shade of the line of figs, then out into the sunshine again.

The boys' cricket game was in recess. The players clustered about a table set out with drinks. Laughter rang across the grass. Briony let her breath out and laughed softly. That feeling of panic was ridiculous. Even if it was Barry Ford—so what? He probably couldn't give a darn about a girl who had turned up for one night and caused an upset in his nice, organised life. If she happened to run into him and he recognised her—all she had to say was: 'Hi—I'm glad I've run into you. I meant to say thanks properly for the hamburger and the loan of your coat.' Something like that. She laughed again. How stupid to build something up into a ... she turned to look behind her.

A horse and rider appeared, the man's headgear flashing white and the animal sheening black as they emerged from the fig trees' canopy. The man reined in for a moment and Briony forgot all her casual greetings and common sense and ran. The sound of hooves on the turf behind her sent her flying, heart racing faster than her feet towards the tree-shrouded gully that marked the creek's course. It hadn't seemed this far when she had sauntered up from the golf course—but at last she reached the outer trees, her breathing and the horse's thunder loud in her ears, or was that just her pulse?

It wasn't. A dark shape passed her, cut in, the horse wheeling in a tight half circle as if it was still in the game. Briony changed direction, made a dash for the narrow bridge, but the pony cut her off again. She was confronted with a close view of a sweating, satiny hide and one booted leg thrust into the stirrup. Panting, she threw back her head. There was no need for her to see the piercing blue of his eyes to confirm that it was him. She had felt it, just as she had felt his presence when she was singing in the band, she had known this man was close. Breathing raggedly, she made a move away but he leaned down and grabbed her arm. Briony stared up at him—she'd known. He had dropped into her mind as soon as she reached the bridge.

'So it is you,' he said curtly. 'Why the hell did you run?' But she had no breath to answer that—and had no answer anyway. Her hair swirled around her face as she shook her head. Why had she?

'What are you doing here, Briony? I thought you were going back to Sydney with your boyfriend—or boyfriends perhaps I should say.'

He frowned down at her. Briony fought to regain her breath and pulled against his grip, but he somehow managed to dismount without letting her go. The sun patched gilded bronze across his face but his eyes burned blue from the visor strip of shadow under his headgear. The boys had resumed their cricket game again and a spatter of applause filtered through the trees. But that sun-drenched field might have been miles away. Here in the dappled shade with the murmur of the creek under the bridge, Briony found herself studying the fine coating of dust that paled the dark chest hair showing in the man's open shirt—he moved to drop the reins and hold her with both gloved hands and she saw the ripple of movement in his neck and shoulders. The pony whickered softly next to them and the sound brought Briony's head up.

'What are you doing here and where are you staying?' he asked again and the peremptory tone restored her.

'Why do you want to know? Are some of your teaspoons missing?' He half smiled at that. 'Maybe I should check them. Though where you would have concealed them in that costume of yours I can't think.'

'Oh heavens, I don't bother with that. I just pass them out the window to all those scruffy, indecent friends of mine,' she said and he frowned at her sarcasm.

'What are you doing here, Briony?' he insisted giving her a little shake. How easy to say she had a job—but he would want to know where and the thought of him knowing panicked her. He might speak to Mrs Gordon. . . .

'I'm working here for a while,' her eyes darted about evasively. 'Then I'll go back to the city.'

'You're certainly not singing in a band then—just exactly what work are you doing?'

He really expected to hear something out of the ordinary, she thought angrily.

'Well what would you expect? Naturally I'm up to no good. A bit of breaking and entering. Stocklea is just full of little old ladies alone in their houses. All those antiques and silver . . . you know what we pop musicians are like—gigs just don't pay enough these days. . . .' The silly words rattled from her and she expected to see irritation, disbelief on his face. Expected him to brush them aside and demand the truth. Instead he gripped her upper arms tight, nearly lifting her feet from the ground.

'I hope that's one of your fairy-tales,' he muttered, close to her face. 'Where are the rest of this band of yours?' He made them sound like a band of thieves instead of musicians.

'Lurking about—casing the place I suppose,' she said flippantly to cover her disturbance at his closeness.

'I can't believe everything you say,' he said at last.

'No!' Briony exclaimed in mock astonishment.

'But I guess there's a germ of truth there somewhere.'

'Maybe I'm just a polished liar,' she suggested, feeling much more in control of herself at last.

'I think you are. But which side of you is the lying side?' he murmured. His hands moved slightly, moulding her shoulders, thumbs feeling for the hollows beneath her collarbone. 'Tell me where you're staying Briony,' he said in a low voice, 'I want to see you again.'

She swallowed, made an attempt to get this meeting back on to any other kind of footing. 'So you can guide me on to the straight and narrow?' she enquired cheekily, tossing back her hair and looking up at him. His mouth twisted into a smile and there was a sensuous quality to it that wiped the confidence from Briony's face. One leather-gloved hand went to her hair as it had that night.

'I fear any path I take with you Briony is unlikely to be straight or narrow.'

'Let me go,' she said, eyes wide and locked to his.

'You don't want that. I can tell. You want what I want, Briony. . . .' His gaze dropped to her mouth and as he lowered his head, she knew he was right. The truth of it rushed at her degradingly. But this time she would not stand waiting like a mesmerised mouse. Her free hand groped about for the horse's damp warmth until she found a leather strap. A sharp pull on it brought a whinny from the animal and its sudden snorting shuffle was enough to loosen the man's hold on her.

Someone called from the direction of the cricket field. It sounded something like 'Baron' but must have been 'Barry' for the man answered as he grabbed the reins and calmed the horse.

'Briony——' he called once, but she was over the bridge and running like a champion to the anonymity of the golf club's car park. Just to be on the safe side she didn't go at once to Amy Gordon's car. The shiny dark blue sedan could easily be identified, she reasoned.

Instead she lurked, heart hammering where she would not be seen. But the man never emerged from the trees. Detained it seemed by whoever had called him. She was safe. But from what?

Fifteen minutes later Mrs Gordon looked at her flushed, tousled appearance.

'My dear girl you look as if you've run a mile. Have you been mowing the lawn?'

'No. I thought I'd do that tomorrow morning. While I was waiting for you I went for a walk and saw a polo game—or rather polocrosse I think it was. I'm afraid I got too close—hence the dust.'

Much too close she thought as the old lady confirmed the existence of the polocrosse club and chattered on about how Doug Drewett played but wasn't nearly as good as Stanford. She talked on about the end of the season and the traditional grudge match ... and playing as a reserve. . . . Briony smiled politely as if she was listening. In reality her mind was way back there, with a tall man who had ridden into her life again and tilted her new, sweet existence. And now she had the wierdest conviction that today wasn't the last she had seen of him. It filled her with foreboding and, she admitted reluctantly, a fiery excitement that no amount of psychic cold water could douse.

'. . . such a thoughtful boy,' Mrs Gordon went on and Briony dragged her mind back. This must be the favourite nephew she was talking about. Again.

'When you meet him, don't worry if he seems a little stand-offish. He can be a bit hard to get along with sometimes—Stanford expects so much of himself, and others. But I'm sure he'll like you.'

'The lady doth protest too much . . .' Briony thought, apprehensive about the hard-to-get-along-with nephew whose opinion mattered more to Amy Gordon than she admitted. 'Margot tells me that Stanford is coming down in the next few days. He tried to phone me apparently when he came back from his trip. Margot has the most remarkable grapevine.'

As they drove the old lady frowned and her lined hand drummed on the glove box.

'Something worrying you, Mrs Gordon?'

'Mmmm? Oh—well its stupid I suppose. And Margot might be quite wrong. Or,' she said thoughtfully, 'she might just have told me to put me off at the sixteenth hole.' It amused Briony that the only place Amy tolerated her niece was on the golf course. And even then it was a shaky tolerance.

'And after all—he's a grown man. If he wants to go falling out of planes again I suppose he knows what he's doing.'

'Falling out of——' Briony laughed. 'That sounds a bit drastic.'

'Stanford used to do a lot of it once—parachuting. His old group are short of a man just when some television team wants to do a documentary on them, so he's going to get back into training. Or so Margot says.' She sighed. 'Of course it might all be nonsense—she wouldn't have spoken to Stanford himself because he's been away. But I have to admit she's not often wrong. At least I suppose it would mean he'd spend a few weekends down here and goodness knows he needs some relaxation. Though how relaxing it would be I don't know—jumping off planes.' She shook her head.

'It must be exciting,' Briony said. An odd hobby though even for a former sportsman. Now where, recently had she seen or heard something about parachuting——? Briony frowned as she turned into Mrs Gordon's drive. Something was niggling away in the recesses of her mind just out of reach. What was it?

CHAPTER FOUR

The feeling of foreboding stayed with her, the new appearance of the man and her nervousness at getting the once-over from Mrs Gordon's nephew blending to jangle her nerves.

But morning made a mock of her worries. A few fluffy clouds floated benign in endless blue, Victor's trilling joined that of the wild birds and Briony fetched the mower from the shed to do the chore Mrs Gordon had insisted on postponing.

'Wait until you're hale and hearty again,' she had said and Briony found out why as she began to push the machine over the thick grass. Mrs Gordon didn't believe in power motors. 'Too noisy—and too many fumes' she maintained. The machine was stream-lined—smooth running, oiled and maintained as it had been by her meticulous predecessor. It is efficient. But it required large amounts of energy to operate. Her energy. Even so, perspiring and shoulders beginning to ache, Briony looked over the velour-smooth patch of lawn she'd cut and breathed the stuff of dreams. New-mown grass and roses. She had actually achieved it.

Head down, she started again, ruefully reflecting that the lawn could turn into a two-day affair at this rate. It was satisfying, though, watching the rough turn to smooth, guiding the mower around the stone-edged garden beds and boots . . . boots? Briony stopped, her chin almost level with the mower handle at this stage of her exertions, and looked at the square-toed boots set in her way. A warning shot its way up her spine and exploded in her brain as she slowly lifted her head to meet eyes that flamed blue in a bronze face.

Eyes that burned like ice on the skin.

'Oh no,' she said on an indrawn breath.

'Oh yes,' he smiled unpleasantly and Briony glanced

towards the house to see Mrs Gordon hurrying down the front steps.

'What are you doing here?' she asked. How had he found her?

'Stanford—how wonderful to see you.' The little woman was clasped briefly in his arms and he kissed her cheek. Stanford? Briony heard the voice coming from miles away. 'You're doing a beautiful job of the lawn, Briony, my dear. I want you to meet my nephew—Stanford Barron, Briony Wilde.'

Skydiving. The book behind glass in a mellow room. The lingering itch at the back of her mind was scratched at last—too late. Stanford—Ford and a first name not a last. Barron *not* Barry. Had she opened the glass door in his study she might have seen the name on the trophies—trophies! All that talk about Stanford the sportsman should have alerted her. She chilled under Ford Barron's blue gaze. He wasn't going to let her stay here. Not the girl who'd caused such a ruckus. The girl who had gone out of her way to show him how tough she was—how itinerant her way of life. Briony felt as if she had fallen from a plane.

'Don't look so apprehensive, Briony,' Mrs Gordon reassured her and patted her arm. Ford followed the affectionate gesture with thoughtful eyes. 'I know Stanford looks as if he's about to bite but I'm afraid that's only because he overworks.'

Ford turned his attention back to his aunt. 'You can't accuse me of that this time, Amy. I'm taking a few days off. I have a jump later today—I daresay Margot has spread the word about that. And yesterday,' his eyes wandered to Briony, 'I played in the last polocrosse game of the season.'

'The grudge match? Well for goodness sake, Briony might have actually seen you in action then. She saw some of the game.'

Ford smiled knowingly. She had certainly seen him in action'.

'I wouldn't like Miss Wilde to think that yesterday was my usual form. I can play a much tougher game.' Satisfied with Briony's quick swallow, he went on: 'So this is Harry's replacement?'

'Now Stanford, I know you'll think it unusual to hire a girl, but it's working out just fine.'

'I confess to being surprised when I found out this morning that you had a gardener called Briony.' With a steely glance at Briony he added, 'And delighted.'

Amy Gordon seemed taken aback. 'Delighted?'

'That you've found help so quickly,' he said smoothly.

'I daresay you'll want to have a chat with Briony,' the old lady said, 'Will you come inside—or——?'

'No. I'd rather like to see what Miss Wilde has made of the caravan. We'll have our little chat there.'

'Well then come on up to the house when you've finished, Stanford. I want to have a word with you about this free-flying.'

'Free-fall, Amy.' He corrected smilingly and took Briony's elbow in an agonising grip and began to walk with her across the lawn.

'Tell me, Miss Wilde,' he said conversationally, 'what decided you on a job in the country?'

Once out of his aunt's sight, his stride lengthened and Briony almost ran alongside him until they reached the van. 'Inside,' he snapped and she went up the steps like a shot, rubbing her elbow.

'Won't you sit down, Mr——' she began foolishly hoping to take over behind social convention.

'Little old ladies alone with with antiques and silver,' he rasped.

She heard her own stupid words and gave a tremulous laugh. 'Oh—I only said that—it was just—'

'That was the germ of truth wasn't it? Because here you are, Briony, nicely established right beside a veritable treasure trove and the owner already treating you more like family than an employee.'

'No, Mr Barron. You're wrong.'

'I wish to God I was. But this little set-up has all the hallmarks of a group effort. It has to be more than coincidence that you were all down here a fortnight ago—was that the "casing" you joked about?' He took her arm and jerked her towards him, staring down at her with a clenched jaw. Just as angrily he thrust her away again and looked around the van, noticing the painting and the plant in its exotic copper bowl. 'I see you've made a start.'

'Of course we were all down here. That was how I was able——' Briony caught up with his accusation. 'Your aunt gave me the bowl—she pressed it on me but I'll give it back. The painting is mine—not from your aunt's walls if that's what you're thinking.'

He looked dispassionately at her. 'Give me one good reason why you are here, mowing lawns and pruning roses. A girl like you doesn't do that because she likes fresh air.' He paused. 'Or maybe she does.'

Briony felt the stab of hurt at that 'a girl like you'. It was her own fault. Mostly, anyway.

'Is this simply a refuge between bands? Or have you maybe made a miscalculation and left it too late to take the easy way out?'

'What are you talking about?' she stared, baffled.

His eyes roved her slim body in the rough jeans, the shirt hanging loose over them. 'It figures. The fainting that night. You're pregnant, is that it?'

Briony's mouth dropped open.

'And you want a nice little place to . . .' he stopped as her colour fled. The high pink of her cheeks turned to chalk. A muscle twitched in his cheek. 'Come now, don't let's have any pretence, Briony. Your private affairs are no concern of mine, but I won't stand by and let you wheedle your way into my aunt's affection so that you can——'

Anger overrode her shock. Briony took a pace forward and swung her arm. His hand snapped out to her wrist, stopping it just a fraction short of his face.

Through her rage she registered a certain surprise in his eyes but all she could think was that everything was ruined. It would be only hours before she was packed off to the city again to the old way of life that seemed so distant here. Deep inside she was crying already at the loss. Irrelevantly she thought that she wouldn't even get to finish the lawn. She tried to pull free of his grip but he held her firmly, pulling her forward so that she was close enough to smell the clean combination of after shave and fine wool. It reminded her of the night she'd worn his jacket, when he'd threaded his fingers in her hair. Around her wrist his hand was hard, hurting—yet a hundred other messages raced along her nerves from his touch. She wanted to run—she wanted to feel his hand in her hair again—she wanted to cry.

Ford Barron let her go. 'Sorry,' she said in a low voice that shook a little. It should be him apologising. 'You're quite wrong. The only reason I'm here is because I needed a job and the city was becoming too——' she broke off as he moved away and leaned against the refrigerator, his head tilted to one side as he watched her, '—expensive. My car was reduced to scrap in an accident, my rent kept going up and I couldn't get permanent work and then I saw this job advertised. With a caravan it said. And quiet, restful surroundings . . .' she stopped. Pointless to try to make him understand the lure of those simple words, the odd conviction she'd had that they meant something special to her.

'Very poignantly played, Briony,' he said dryly. 'I'm almost tempted to give the silver futures a miss and invest in your career as an actress. You have a nice touch for soap opera.'

His cynical tones released her temper. She had told the truth and had it ridiculed. Darn the man! Couldn't he recognise sincerity when he saw it?

'I wouldn't advise you to invest in anything that required accurate observation, Mr Barron,' she retorted. 'You'd lose.'

'No. I won't lose. And I don't intend my aunt to lose either. So I advise you to tread very carefully. She seems to have developed an affection for you—but that doesn't matter. If I find you taking advantage of her you'll be out of your ear.'

'Look, Mr Barron, I haven't done anything to earn your distrust.'

'Let's keep it that way then, because I'm warning you, if there is an item of my aunt's missing at any time I'll have you and your colleagues in custody before you have time to tune a guitar.' He paused. 'I take it you didn't tell Amy about your associations with a rock band while you were filling her in on the sad details of your life?'

She flushed. 'No.' Suddenly the tone of the conversation registered with her. 'You'll be out on your ear' he had said, not 'you are out'.

'Do you mean you are letting me stay?'

He shoved his hands into his pockets and watched her.

'That depends.'

'On what, Mr Barron?'

'Several things.' He was looking oddly at her, a shadow—just the faintest shadow—of doubt on his face. Maybe she could convince him after all.

'Mr Barron——' she thought of the long, beautiful days—of fussing, motherly Mrs Gordon and dear George, and her hand went to Ford's sleeve in an unconscious plea. 'I can promise you—if you let me stay on—you won't be sorry.' She looked into his eyes hoping to see some response and she did. But not quite what she expected. Calculation narrowed his gaze. He glanced down at her hand still expressively on his arm.

'Is that so?' he said very softly and the tone told her that he had misunderstood—wildly misunderstood her.

Briony snatched her hand away but before she could step back his arm was about her waist. 'I didn't mean——' she began. Hauled against him, she struggled and kicked to evade the inevitable, to fight the alarming rush of her senses at the warm strength of him, the familiar scent of his skin and the oddly boyish overscent of the wool sweater he wore. Her hands pushed at his chest, pummelled his shoulders. He held her like that, arms steel-curved about her until she gasped, her fists stilled from sheer effort.

'Maybe I misunderstood you,' he admitted surveying her hot, flushed face. Briony stared into the cool-warm depths of his eyes and felt the weakness flood upwards from her knees. Without volition, her body began to melt against his. He felt it. 'Then again, maybe not.'

'Let me go,' she said in new alarm.

'Not the words of an opportunist but let's make sure. . . .'

She didn't see the kiss coming. One moment she was doing her best to break contact with him and the next her head was forced back under the pressure of his mouth. Such was the impact that her hands clutched at his shoulders for support before she renewed her struggles. But they were token. Ford bound her to him and held her head with a hand outspread and tangled in her hair. Then it all changed. The pressure, the force turned to dreamy, silken caresses from that hard mouth. Her desire to escape seemed a childish notion now as her fingers curved over the wool-textured contours of his shoulders, her body surrendered to the wave of weakness that rippled on and on. Ford's lips on hers were a powerful, taunting question and even as she responded, she knew that she was giving the wrong answer. But there was no option. Her lips parted for him and Briony heard the warning drums beat retreat in helplessness.

'Well, well—you do want the job, don't you?'

'I wasn't—you——' How to explain that her response was instinctive, that it had not been offered in exchange for her job? She couldn't understand it herself, let alone explain it. Frustration boiled up in her. She didn't even like the man!

'Either you want to stay here enough to be—pleasant to me, because you know don't you, Briony, that I could have you thrown out very quickly? Or——' he gave a sardonic smile, 'I would have to put your enthusiasm down to my own incredible expertise.'

Abruptly he let her go and she stepped back.

'Being a modest man I really feel I must take the first as the most likely.'

'You—you're contemptible,' she almost whispered.

Ford's mouth hardened. 'I think you'll find I can be even more contemptible if necessary.' He tugged the lower edge of his sweater into place and watched her run shaking hands over her falling hair. As he stepped outside she realised that she still didn't know for sure.

'Wait.' He turned back. The sun sat golden on one

broad shoulder, texturing the fabric of his sweater and touching tentatively at the severe lines of his face.

'Am I to stay—will you tell Mrs Gordon to fire me?'

Ford regarded her, his head thrown back and eyes half closed. As if he was weighing her future. Which he probably was.

A flash of anger banished the confusion that cottonballed in her head.

'I think you've earned a trial period,' he mused. 'But you may have to do better if you want to stay permanently.'

'Just say yes or no, Mr Barron. If there is any question of paying for my job in a similar vein, I'll pack right now.'

'You "paid" quite willingly I thought. However I was referring to your other performance—of the duties for which you were hired. From what I can see you haven't been doing a great deal.'

'In that case, Mr Barron, you can be assured that on your next visit you'll be completely satisfied.'

'Ah—I see you've grasped the situation, Briony. That's *exactly* what I expect. To be completely satisfied.'

He certainly appeared content with her silence. With the last word safely in his corner he turned and went, heels clicking decisively on the flagging. And Briony watched him go, wondering if he was just playing with words—or with her.

Whatever he said to his aunt must have been fairly noncommittal for Mrs Gordon merely said that Stanford had 'reservations' about a girl being fit for the job. Reservations. In all fairness she had to admit that he was justified to some extent. She had made the wrong impression from the start and something told her that to deny now all that silly posturing as Cheryl would be useless. She had let him—encouraged him to—keep his prepackaged ideas of a roving, unwholesome life and it was too late now simply to say it was not true. But proving herself willing to work was one thing. She felt she was doing a fair job of that in spite of his sarcastic disclaimer. Proving herself honest and trustworthy was going to be nigh impossible as she discovered nearly a week after his first 'inspection'.

Her first maintenance job had come up. Nothing too onerous. A picture hook in the lounge room wall. Briony smiled brightly when Mrs Gordon asked her to do it but the simple task had a worrying aspect.

'I want to hang this painting over the cabinet here,' the old lady said, showing her the spot. 'I'm sure Harry had a supply of picture hooks in the tool box. But be careful when you hammer it in won't you? He did say that these old walls could crack easily.'

Oh lord, Briony thought, dreading the elementary task of tapping in a nail through the hook. She could almost see a great crack running like lightning up to the picture rail and beyond—and that would do her reputation no good with Mr Barron. After Briony had driven Mrs Gordon to her Saturday golf, she found Harry's tool box and went into the house with twofold reluctance. First because of the risk of damaging the wall and second, because even with permission she was uneasy inside the house after all Ford Barron's warnings.

As it happened, her trepidation about the first was unnecessary. The picture hook was held in place and a fine nail tapped with exquisite care through it. Briony sighed, put the hammer in the tool box and dragged her moist hands down her overalls. Not a sign of a crack. Pleased, she picked up the painting and leaned over the cabinet to hang it. As the picture wire connected with the hook, the cabinet shuddered and something inside fell over. 'Damn,' she muttered and crouched down to see what it was. The shelves of the glass-fronted case were crammed with porcelain and glass and bronze. Her eyes ran along past an Oriental figurine, several crystal items and a small framed etching that stood against the back wall of the cabinet. One tiny cold-rimmed coffee cup was rocking gently beside its saucer. Thankful that it hadn't broken, she opened the doors and lifted out the cup to inspect it for chips. It was unmarked and she ran a finger around the almost transparent edge of the beautiful object.

'It's not worth a great deal alone,' a bone-dry voice said behind her. 'You'd need the set to make it worth your while.'

She nearly dropped the cup, so startled was she. Still kneeling she twisted to see Ford Barron looking down at her, his eyes cool with suspicion. He must have a key, for he was entering from the front hall.

'I was just checking for chips,' she said defensively.

'Such devotion to duty. Do you intend to check *all* my aunt's belongings for possible flaws?'

His gaze moved about the room rather as it had that night when she'd hidden a sandwich behind her. Now, as then, he was obviously wondering what she might have taken.

'I bumped the cabinet and knocked it over,' she explained.

'Amy's out, I gather. What are you doing in the house?' The painting, hanging crookedly on its hook attracted his attention. 'Looking for a safe perhaps?'

'What?' She followed his eyes and saw what he meant. Angrily she straightened the frame.

'No. I came in to put a hook on the wall so that your aunt could hang the picture. She asked me to do it but as she won't be back for a couple of hours I'm afraid you can't verify that with her right now. But there's the tool box.'

Ford Barron checked her over minutely, taking in every detail of the bright blue overalls she wore over a shirt, her dark hair, bouncy and shining and bound in post-shampoo desperation into two pigtails.

'That doesn't prove a thing.'

'Well I can't help that,' she snapped, flustered by the way his eyes were roving. 'Maybe you'd like to search me?'

The lightning blue eyes did another swift reconnaissance. 'Maybe I would at that,' he agreed softly and in the hush that fell between them the ormolu clock's ticking was loud and important. He moved and Briony rushed to pick up the tool box, backing away with all speed which was difficult in this room where wine tables, footstools and lampstands competed for space with the chairs.

She was defeated by a pianola leg in the end and only a familiar firm hand about her arm prevented her from stumbling with the tools.

'Mr Barron, I haven't taken a thing. Not,' she flung at him, 'even a sandwich.'

He put up a hand, lightly touched one of her pigtails. 'You look about seventeen,' he said slowly. 'And I could easily believe butter wouldn't melt in your mouth if I didn't know——'

Was that a trace of regret in his trailed-off words? Briony hoped it was the first sign of doubt.

'Mr Barron, I'm not what you think, really. I know I said a lot of silly things but that was just—I don't know—bravado.' She hoped he wouldn't ask why she'd needed a show of bravado. 'And I'm not dishonest.'

'You've overdone it again, Briony.' His voice was dry. 'The squeaky clean hair and pigtails were enough—the soulful plea in those big hazel eyes is pure over-acting.'

'Oh—you——' she choked. 'I'm not acting at all.'

'Then tell me where you went that Saturday night when you left my house—and keep that virtuous look in your eyes while you do it.' She was immediately evasive and he noted it with a sardonic smile.

'I told you where I was going. To wait by the gate for Jeff to come back for me. He was going to drop me off at Stocklea on his way back to Sydney.'

'And did he?' His eyes were intent as she nodded. 'Where did you stay? And I might warn you that I checked with the hotel and know it wasn't there. Where did you go—dressed as Wonder Woman, with no means of transport?'

She could tell him where she stayed but it made her sound too much the vagrant. Instead she shrugged her refusal to discuss it.

'Ah, I see. Someone else accommodated you perhaps. You had one offer in my study.'

His or Neil's did he mean? 'Two offers if you recall, Mr Barron. Neither appealed to me.'

'At least I know which one you didn't take,' he rasped apparently angered over it.

'You don't know anything, Mr Barron.'

'Neither did your friend Jeff. How did you manage to keep your whereabouts secret from your very affectionate bandleader?'

'My very affectionate bandleader is my brother, Mr Barron.'

His brows went up and after a moment so did the temperature. In a warmer tone he said: 'Of course. Wilde. I didn't take too much notice of your last name. I should have connected it with his.'

'That's one boyfriend you can cross off my list,' she told him tartly.

'What's the saying, Briony, "plenty more fish in the sea"!'

'Oh——' she spluttered, 'Go—jump out of a plane why don't you?'

He smiled. Actually smiled. 'With pleasure. But both my chutes will be in perfect condition, so I'll be back.'

'Do let me know when your next inspection is due. Will you need to search my quarters perhaps?'

'Is that an invitation, Briony?'

She made it to the door, weighed down by the tool box and shook her head briskly. The pigtails flipped against her face. 'You know it isn't. But you can be sure that if you should arrive uninvited, there'll be nothing, absolutely nothing there out of place.'

Ford pushed back the edges of the zippered jacket he wore and set his hands on his hips. 'Yes there will. You. You are out of place, Briony Wilde, and I'll find out why.' He looked again at the cabinet, walked over and lifted the picture from the wall and his snort of laughter stopped her as she began to leave.

'At least I can believe that you put up this hook. It won't hold more than a few hours as it is. Give me the hammer.' He held out a commanding hand to her.

'What's wrong with it?' she protested, all her pleasure in a simple task well done spoiled.

'The nail is barely in.' One twitch and it came off easily. 'See. It requires a longer nail driven in further. You're no expert are you, Briony? Not at your job, anyway.'

She came over and he took the hammer and a longer nail from the tool box.

'But the reason I didn't hit it too hard was...' she started to say when he raised the hammer and struck several times sharply. A jagged crack appeared like magic, streaking upwards for several feet.

Silence.

'... because Mrs Gordon said the wall might crack,' she finished.

Ford stared at the result of his handiwork and after a moment Briony stifled a giggle. She reached out and took the hammer from him, returned it to the tool box with a flourish. 'Well that hook certainly looks a *great* deal more secure, Mr Barron,' she said brightly. 'But its just not your day is it? If I were you, I'd check my parachutes *very* carefully today.'

She left feeling rather cheerful which was awful of her she supposed considering Mrs Gordon's wall was spoiled. But a bit of putty or something would fix that. Meanwhile she could enjoy the closest look to dismay that she might ever see on Ford Barron's face. If she could have whistled, she would have.

Later of course, her pleasure dimmed. Her days here could be numbered with him breathing down her neck just waiting for her to make a wrong move and misinterpreting even the right ones. But at least if he was as overworked as Mrs Gordon hinted, he wouldn't have much time to dog her footsteps. Briony shelved the baffling question of her responses to his kiss. There was no logic she could apply to that. She found a library book that explained how to patch up cracks in walls and ceilings. If only, she thought, all repair work was as simple.

'That's not like Stanford,' Mrs Gordon told Briony as she plastered the wall on Monday. 'Not like him to make a mess of things.'

'Hmmm,' said Briony.

She bought herself a cheap planter for the prayer plant so that she could give back the bowl to Mrs Gordon. If Ford Barron called again he would find none of his aunt's treasures in her van.

'Sorry about this,' she muttered as she took the plant into the annexe in its glorious copper bowl. 'Think of it as a luxury holiday in a penthouse.' She lifted it out and put it in the cane planter. 'Holiday over—this is home for you from now on, humble but all yours.'

'Do you talk to your plant too?' said a delighted Amy as she came up behind her. 'George thinks I'm an old eccentric but I believe it works.'

Briony grinned, thinking of Amy's sun-room jungle. 'I believe it too,' she said and gave her back the copper bowl. 'Thanks for the loan, Mrs Gordon.'

'Oh aren't we independent,' the old lady said and took it.

The hectic pace Briony set brought a healthy glow to her cheeks. She ate big breakfasts that had seemed nauseating in the city and her jeans began to sit snugly on her hips. Her meagre bank account showed figures in the double column for a change, even after she'd resignedly sent off another instalment on the ill-fated car. Only five more months and she would own the ghost of the little V.W. Twice she rang Jeff to let him know how her job was progressing but without really knowing why, omitted to mention the identity of Mrs Gordon's favourite nephew.

Jeff was bursting with achievement. Silverhero had got their contract for an eight-week country tour and Jeff's only problem was finding a replacement for Duane, who had left to take an unlikely job in a restaurant's resident band.

'Pretty up-market from what I hear,' Jeff said, 'I believe our Duane wears a frilled shirt and even got his hair cut for the job. He'll need to trim his temper as well.'

'Have you anyone else in mind to play lead?'

'A few. Not as good as Duane but I daresay a lot less trouble. Having that guy around was like living with an unexploded grenade in your pocket.'

He remained sceptical about her job. 'You can use my flat, Bry—while I'm on tour. If you get sick of trimming Mrs Thingammy's carnations. I'll send you the key.'

'Thanks a lot, but not necessary. And if that was a trap for me—it failed. You don't trim carnations.'

'Tch, tch. August already and you haven't trimmed your carnations?' Jeff exclaimed.

'You're impossible. Seriously, I'm happy here, Jeff.' She must have sounded too earnest for he said somewhat dryly:

'Take your word for it, Sis.'

'And, Jeff?'

'Yes?'

'Do you have to trim carnations?'

He laughed. 'I think maybe I'd better send you that key.'

George Olsen dropped in almost every day to see Amy Gordon and soon made a habit of calling at the van for a few minutes. One evening he came around before their twice-weekly game of cards.

'Brought you a book about carnations, Briony,' he said with a perfectly straight face. 'There's a good chapter on collar rot.'

'So you should, after pretending to Mrs Gordon that I knew something about it.' Briony took the battered book with a smile.

'Would you like some tea, George?'

He shook his head. 'I'll be having some with Amy in a while. To tell you the truth,' he looked over his shoulder, 'before I go up to the house what I would like is to——' he tapped the outline of his pipe in his top pocket.

'By all means light up. I'm sure I've got an oxygen mask about somewhere.'

Chuckling he filled the pipe and lit it. A powerful smell was released in the van but Briony found it rather pleasant. Homey.

'Got yourself nicely set up here, Briony, my dear,' he nodded approval at the spotless van, warm with her few possessions. Inclining his head towards the double bed that was partly concealed behind its curtain he said: 'That's more like it, eh?'

It was all he said about her night spent on the hard bench of the railway station Ladies' and Briony knew he would not tell the story to anyone else. 'Mum's the word' he'd said to her when she got the job. Retired,

George worked only a few nights a week. It had been her good fortune that he had been on duty that night, Briony thought.

'George Olsen——' a firm voice said from the van steps, 'I have a pot of tea, Irene, Fred and a pack of cards waiting.'

'Hello, Amy. Did you follow the sound of voices?'

'No. I followed my nose.' Amy Gordon's lined face crinkled further as she grimaced. 'That darned pipe of yours, George, is disgusting. One day I'll get hold of it and toss it on the compost heap. Briony won't be able to breathe in here tonight.'

'Oh it's all right, Mrs Gordon, honestly. I'm from the city and used to pollution.'

The old lady laughed. 'Come on, George, and kill that fire before you get near the house. Join us for a game of cards, Briony, my dear?'

It was tempting, even though she knew nothing whatever about cards. There was a warmth about these two that made her long to be with them—as if they were family. But she had to guard against her yearnings to belong. That might lead her to step too far outside her role of employee and would be quickly mis-interpreted by Mr Ford Barron.

'Thank you but I think I'll just——'

'Play your guitar?' Mrs Gordon prompted. 'We heard you the other night. Lovely my dear. We'll leave the windows open and listen to you.'

'Do you do requests?' George wanted to know and chuckled as he tapped out his pipe in the garden. 'How about "Smoke Gets in your Eyes"?'

With her finances improving, Briony let her head go and bought some jeans and a super, irresistible, entirely unsuitable dress. Just where she would wear it here in her new outdoors life she had no idea, but as she draped its jade sheened fabric across her in the caravan, she didn't care. It was gorgeous and showed off her dark hair and tan. The neckline was a deep vee and it fitted everywhere it should and hinted at everything else. Just once, she found herself thinking, it would be nice if he could see her in this. He had never seen her looking her best. Just sequins and boots, jeans and overalls. In this, with her hair swept up so—and high, high heels—Briony caught herself dreaming. She bundled the garment on to a hanger and shut it firmly into the wardrobe, annoyed with the drift of her thoughts. With a bit of luck he would be swamped with work and not come down here for months in which case he wouldn't see her at all. Nor she—him. That was something to wish for.

But she should have known, her wishes rarely came true. In fact when Amy Gordon told her that Ford was taking his first holidays in years—coming down to stay in his house for an unprecedented three weeks, she wasn't altogether surprised. Her growing uneasiness in an otherwise cloudless existence was a sure sign that he would soon be back. But for three weeks! That was a blow. Was the man going to be coming by continually, criticising and waving the sword of Damocles over her head? And making nonsense of her theory that sheer physical attraction was a fallacy?

His aunt at least was delighted. 'I've been trying to talk him into a good long break for years and had no success. He needs to relax. If only he'd go back to golf instead of this free-flying—free-fall.'

Briony felt like saying that she didn't think he could relax whatever he did. That frown was a permanent fixture and so, apparently, was his suspicious nature.

Stanford's tendency to overwork made his aunt cluck all over again. 'My brother left the business in a shaky state when he developed heart trouble and Stanford has built it up through sheer hard work. Ted was lucky he had him to take over.'

'Is Ted your brother?'

'Yes, Stanford's Dad. He and Liz live in Europe now and only because Stanford runs everything so well. If they'd had to rely on Stuart things would have been different.' She saw Briony's curious look at the name. 'He's Stanford's younger brother—plays drums in a band.'

So his brother played in a band. Why then was he so disparaging about pop musicians? Briony longed to ask about Stuart but Mrs Gordon had gone on to deplore Stanford's inability to find 'some nice girl' and settle down. She could have offered one or two reasons for that. But didn't.

The weather was indulgent, the air pure and scented as Briony began Mrs Gordon's rose pruning. She would have been content, but for the stretching of her nerves as she found herself listening for the throaty roar of a car engine and a deep voice full of cynicism.

She heard both only days later. But not in that order.

CHAPTER FIVE

IT was another cloudless day—not warm—but for Briony who was distributing the compost established by the redoubtable Harry—warm enough. When the boy from the local garage brought Amy's car back after replacing the radiator hose, Briony was flushed and grubby, her jeans rolled up to her knees and a T-shirt clinging to her figure.

Dave, nineteen and bursting with inoffensive ego, had tried his amusing line on her before and was doing so again with a good-humoured acceptance that he would fail as usual. But Briony laughed at his outrageous flattery, even as she carefully checked the new hose, mindful that it was her responsibility to see that Mrs Gordon got what she paid for.

'Have a drink with me tonight, Briony? Come on, what have you got against younger men?'

'Younger men? I'll bet you're not even old enough to go into the hotel yet.'

'Sure I am. Is it a date then? Drinks tonight?'

She laughed again as she closed the hood. 'The hose looks okay,' she said to Dave's disgust, 'Just make sure Mrs Gordon is charged the right amount if you know what I mean. . . .' She felt a prickle of awareness on the back of her neck and swung around. Ford Barron stood right behind them, looking as immaculate as they did grubby, enigmatic in sunglasses.

'And do you know what she means?' he asked Dave while the blank lenses stayed fixed on Briony. It was a moment before she saw what he was getting at.

'Yeah, sure. Briony found a mistake in the last account and she means—um—be more careful.' Dave was unnerved by Ford's unfriendly presence. 'I'll walk back, Briony. See you.'

Briony counted to ten. 'Contrary to your worst suspicions, Mr Barron, I don't have a little arrangement with the garage to overcharge your aunt and split the difference. That was what was on your mind?'

She could just make out his eyes moving behind the glasses.

'It would be the easiest thing in the world to organise,' he said. 'My aunt is very—trusting.'

'It doesn't run in the family apparently,' she said shortly. 'I'm amazed anyone as untrusting as you can have faith in something as fragile as a parachute.'

'I wouldn't—not unless I'd checked it out personally first,' he told her smoothly.

'Mr Barron—I'm sure you're a busy man. There's really no need for you to go on checking me out personally. I'm not pinching things from your aunt's house, or embezzling her. I've been here for weeks and nothing terrible has happened.'

'There are other ways of cheating. Standing about flirting for instance, instead of doing the jobs you were hired for. I hope that wasn't a date you made for tonight. My aunt may want you to drive her to my place.'

Briony gaped. 'Flirting? I wasn't.'

He looked sceptical and she rushed on, angry and anxious to justify herself. Hadn't she worked like a fiend since he was here last?

'You've no right to say I've neglected my work.' She flung out a hand at the garden. 'Tell me what I haven't done that my predecessor would have.'

'You don't really want to know, Briony, do you? You've found yourself a nice little sinecure here with a few possibilities on the side. I've made some enquiries about your brother's band and wasn't surprised to find that one of them has a record. But I warn you again, don't think you'll get away with cheating my aunt in any way.'

Duane, she thought. It had to be Duane with a record. He was the wild one. She wondered if Jeff knew and doubted it. At least he had left the band now—did Mr Barron know that too?

'I wouldn't cheat Mrs Gordon if I was starving,' she said.

He took off the sun lenses and flicked those blue eyes over her. 'But you were starving weren't you?' he reminded her.

Briony looked down at her sneakered feet, frustrated and despairing of ever convincing this man that she was genuine. As he moved away she looked up. 'Tell me.' She caught his arm and dropped it when he looked down at her grubby hand on his immaculate jacket sleeve. 'Tell me exactly where I haven't measured up.' And of course she regretted it. She had known that Amy Gordon was protecting her from some of the heavier work but it was worse than she thought.

'The eaves are due for cleaning—cobwebs—you see, there and there.' He pointed them out. 'The front fence requires mending in three places. I'm surprised you haven't noticed. Harry would have.' His unemotional voice ran on and Briony's heart sank. 'And of course the fig tree is due to be lopped. Harry attended to it each winter.' He looked down into her crestfallen face. 'So you see you are really rather a luxury, aren't you Briony. If you want to stay here I suggest you keep your mind on the few duties you accept as yours and spend less time trifling with the affections of schoolboys.'

He went into the house then and only the later growl of his car as he left eased her frustration.

Briony changed into her new jeans and a frilled shirt to drive Mrs Gordon to Abingdon that evening. Not to impress its owner—merely as a courtesy to her employer. Fervently she hoped it would be a simple matter of dropping the old lady off and coming straight back. The less she saw of the favourite nephew, the better. 'Trifling with the affections of schoolboys' indeed.

'. . . so thoughtful,' Mrs Gordon was saying of him. 'The Colonel is an old, old friend and just passing through. Stanford knew I'd want to see him. He's a dear boy.'

'Hmmm,' said Briony.

Her heart fluttered oddly when she saw the house again. Its old brick glowed warm peach in the shrubbery lights. The wide colonial verandah had a hospitable, welcoming look to it—a quite misleading welcoming look Briony thought, as soon as you pictured its owner framed in the double doors. As if the thought had substance, he appeared there and strolled out across the stone floor to the steps. Close behind him was an elderly man, his face crumpling into a mosaic of lines and parchment skin as he smiled.

'Amy!' he cried and made his deliberate way down the steps, leaning on his stick, to plant a hearty kiss on Mrs Gordon's cheek just as Briony opened the door for her.

'As impetuous as ever, Milly,' she said in the censorious tone she adopted to cover her own fluster. 'Impetuous' was obviously a word that had applied long ago in the Colonel's caneless days.

'This is Briony, Milly. Be careful with that cane.'

The old man nodded to Briony and took Mrs Gordon's arm.

Milly? The old lady saw her puzzlement. 'Milton, my dear—we seemed to form the habit of silly abbreviations in the forties.'

Together they made their way up the steps and Briony heard Milly say, 'You haven't changed a bit Amy.' Her 'Pshaw' spoke volumes of delight. An old admirer perhaps? Briony watched them outlined against the interior glow. Then they were gone and Briony was aware that she, too, was being watched. Ford Barron remained at the top of the steps, arms folded, his body leaning against a pillar. He was wearing a checked shirt and cords with a waistcoat. The soft glow from inside lit his face, softening the hard lines from striking to handsome. Quickly Briony closed the car door.

'Goodnight, Mr Barron,' she said crisply and went around to the driver's side. Before she could get in, he was there beside her trapping her in the open doorspace.

'In a hurry, Briony?'

'Not especially. But there seems no reason to linger. I've done my job,' she added the last sarcastically.

'You could always have a drink before you leave,' he said, 'Unless you're off to drink with your youthful mechanic.'

'I'm not. And though it's awfully democratic of you—no thanks. As staff I don't expect to drink with the family.' She eyed his arm, leaning across the doorway and preventing her entry. 'Now if you'll excuse me, I'm in a hurry.'

'You said you weren't.'

'That was before I had time to reflect. With you in a half-mile radius I'd forgotten—I'm always in a hurry.'

Amazingly, it annoyed him. Grasping her wrist, he said—a trifle thickly, she thought: 'You seem to have forgotten Briony—a few words in my aunt's ear and I can have you out on yours.'

'I haven't forgotten. But you'd better make up your mind quickly because your aunt likes me—and the longer you leave it the more words you'll have to use to dislodge me.' She hadn't meant to but it came out as a taunt and she knew she had created exactly the impression he expected.

'You little——' he muttered. 'I was beginning to think I could be wrong about you, but you really are a cheap little adventuress aren't you?'

Around her wrist his fingers tightened and she gasped, 'Let go—I didn't mean to say that—you make me so angry——'

'Of course you didn't mean to say it. But we know where we stand and that's no bad thing. My first concern is my aunt. I don't want her taken in by a splendid little actress with her eye on the main chance.'

'You——' she clenched her teeth as he caught her other wrist and held her helpless in the angle of the open car door. 'Oh go ahead, do your worst, Mr Barron. I'm tired of wondering every day if you're going to toss me out. Why don't you go ahead and do it. If you can do it.'

'Because another solution has occurred to me,' he said silkily and all her senses were alerted. 'In business there are several ways of dealing with misplaced personnel. And one is the sideways promotion.' His eyes glittered and she felt the lurch of her heart and the start of unwilling weakness in her legs. 'Simply it's a matter of offering another position—one more—suitable.'

'I don't want another . . .' she began when he folded her arms behind her, still grasping her wrists. The move brought her hard against him, silenced her.

'Move back to Sydney. I'll provide you with accommodation.'

So that was it. She felt soiled and sick and bitterly disappointed. He had insulted her, manhandled her and she knew that some of that was her own fault for misleading him. But this—this was contemptible. He despised her yet he was willing to overlook his low opinion of her for the oldest reasons in the world.

'You hypocrite,' she choked.

'Think of the advantages, Briony,' he mocked in a whisper that brushed warm against her lips, then he kissed her, his mouth cool and hard and tasting faintly of whisky, and even after all he had said, Briony heard her pulses begin their thunder in her ears. But she remained passive, unyielding and he raised his head and looked at her through narrowed eyes.

'Mr Barron,' she said in a voice that trembled, 'I would rather scrub the streets of Sydney on my knees than accept your "sideways promotion".' He let her go and she rubbed her wrists. 'And I just wonder what your aunt would think of your offer?'

As if she would ever repeat such a shameful thing Briony thought as she drove away. The road blurred before her and she dashed a hand across her eyes. Everything was getting out of hand. Her peaceful backwater existence had become steadily more complex since that beautiful sunny morning when she first mowed Mrs Gordon's lawn. Leaving seemed the only solution—and the one thing she didn't want. Briony lay awake thinking about it long after she heard the slam of car doors out in the street and the faint murmur of voices that marked Amy Gordon's return with her nephew. And long after the sound of his car left the vast silence of Sandalwood Street, she lay tense, wondering if he would follow up on his proposition. Her vulnerability, both geographic and emotional, loomed large. In midnight illogicality she got up and locked the van door.

She worked harder than ever—the major jobs thrown at her as a challenge by Ford Barron fitted in with Amy Gordon's full social schedule. The old lady protested when she came home from her midweek golf and found Briony had finished the cleaning of the eaves.

'That's heavy work, my dear. Your neck will be sore.'

It was. And her shoulders. And her wrists. Harry no doubt had experienced no such problems.

The fence repairs were more awkward but she asked George's advice next time he dropped by.

'Not tackling that rough work, Briony?' he exclaimed, moving his pipe a fraction.

'Gardening and maintenance is my job, George. I'm afraid I've rather neglected the maintenance part.'

'Amy didn't remind you,' he said shrewdly, his eyes crinkling as pipe smoke rose, 'So it must have been young Ford.'

She didn't answer and George nodded. 'Takes life a bit seriously at times does Ford. Of course he carries a lot of weight on young shoulders. It isn't easy. What do you think of him?'

'It's not what I think that matters, George. Unfortunately I haven't made the right impression on him. I'm an untidy addition to the tidy life he and his family lead.'

George chuckled. 'Things can get a mite too tidy. Ford, I suspect, has been getting a bit bored lately— work that's too tough and pleasure that's too easy.'

'What do you mean?'

'I mean it might be better for him if he could ease up at work and had to try a little harder in his private life. He's wealthy you see and that's a big attraction. And I suppose women might find him good looking—do you think?'

'Oh yes.' Hastily she added, 'Some women would think so.'

George ruminated and several clouds of smoke puffed from his pipe before he removed it and tapped out the contents. 'Make sure you use the galvanised bolts my dear,' he said and pointed them out in Harry's extensive tool box, then ambled in to see Amy.

The fence was duly repaired and Briony was proud of the result. But the last job gave her some grave doubts. She walked round and round the massive fir tree, assessing, planning tactics as if she was scheduled to step into the arena with it. For days she put it off, conscious that her slender strength was no match for the giant. At the bottom of her reluctance were two things. A disinclination to trim anything so majestic and a fear of climbing so far above the ground.

A tentative assault, launched with ladder and handsaw, lasted no more than twenty minutes. In that time she carved the merest stroke on the most offending branch and climbed down again, giddy and exhausted. But this was a fight she couldn't concede. It had been important from the start to show Ford Barron he was wrong. His proposition made it almost an obsession with Briony. And the fig tree became a symbol.

Then she discovered the chainsaw. She considered its possibilities—plugged it in to the cabana power point to try it on a dead lemon branch. It sliced through the timber as if it was bread. Other possibilities occurred to her, the worst that it might slice through her arm with the same ease. But Briony slept on the idea and when Mrs Gordon was safely at a bridge luncheon, she resolutely plugged in an extra-long extension lead and mounted the ladder again with her new super weapon. Stretched out on one thick branch, she felt the familiar nausea and refused to look down.

Three sections, she had decided on. The tip of the branch first, then a strategic withdrawal to dispense with the middle bit and last, the muscular section closest to the trunk. Simple. Just a question of common sense, she assured herself and switched the chainsaw on. It buried its teeth in the branch, shrieking like a banshee and Briony winced at the noise and the powerful pull of the machine. The cord resisted a fraction and she pulled it free, looking down to see Ford Barron through the leaves, mouthing something at her. Her nerves leapt but she kept doggedly on, knowing that a lapse in concentration could be dangerous. The saw wailed and the tip of the branch, almost severed, splintered and began to drop. As it tore free to fall, the loss of its weight jerked the remaining branch upwards and Briony gasped as she pressed the saw's off button and tightened her hold. That was something she hadn't foreseen and the adrenalin pumped through her system.

In the deafening quiet, Ford Barron's voice floated up to her.

'What the hell do you think you're doing? Get down here—now.'

Frightened out of her wits a moment ago, she regained her courage. It was something to do with him standing there watching, she knew.

'Get out of the way. There's a heavy section coming next,' she called and ignored his shouts as she slid backwards and braced herself against the trunk. Once more the chainsaw screeched into timber and Briony panted as she held its hungry, shuddering bulk and kept her balance. 'Luxury' was she? When it was less than halfway through the bough the saw stopped. Frowning she pressed the starter but nothing happened. The saw was firmly stuck in the cut and she almost fell trying to pull it out.

'For God's sake get down here.' A voice bellowed and she looked to see Ford at the tree's base, the extension plug at his feet.

'How dare you unplug it. I was right in the middle of a cut—that could have been dangerous,' she yelled, shaking and giddy as the ground beckoned her.

'Get—DOWN!'

She inched her way to the ladder, screwing up her eyes to stop the dizziness. Halfway down the rungs, she glanced into Ford Barron's upturned face, white with anger, and the fear hit her fully. Oh no——' she groaned as her foot missed the next rung and her weight swung too far out. Not with him here. The ladder began to move but was quickly jammed back against the tree. Briony fell, bracing herself for the jolt of the earth.

Ford broke her fall but staggered under the impact, his foot catching one of the knobbled fig roots that ribbed the ground. They both toppled in an awkward mesh of arms and legs and Ford's breath left him in a grunt as he measured his length across the tree's tortuous root system. Briony sprawled on top of him, her head whirling and she cried out as her knee struck something.

'You bloody little fool!' Ford bit out and turned so that she rolled off him on to the ground. Finding him suddenly looming over her, an arm each side of her body was almost as big a shock as her unplanned descent. His blue eyes fairly blazed down at her and he clenched and unclenched his teeth as if he couldn't find the words for his anger. But of course he did. Briony winced as he blasted her.

'Are you an idiot? What possessed you to use a chainsaw? What are you trying to prove?'

'That I'm a gardener, Mr Barron,' she shouted back, 'And willing to perform my duties.' She pushed the hair from her eyes with a shaking hand and stared up at him, hating him for making her want to prove herself, hating herself for the fiery acknowledgment of his nearness. What flawed chemistry made her come physically alive to a man who looked at her the way he did? She averted her eyes and tried to get up but he held her there on the ground, studying her with a curious expression.

'How long have you been up there using that damned saw?'

'I don't know,' she said wildly, desperate to get up and away from the odd intimacy of the situation. 'Would you like me to keep daily time sheets, Mr Barron?'

'Those tools are heavy—meant to be handled by a man. Good God, Briony, you could have lopped your own arm off, or killed yourself. It's a job for experts, like Harry.'

She lay still, panting a little from her exertions and the belated conviction that she had come close to just that. 'Well, that would have solved all your problems wouldn't it? A one-armed gardener wouldn't keep her job for long would she? And she wouldn't be able to return to her sordid life as a guitarist either.' She began to laugh, her own fears taking awful, possible shape with the shock of the fall. Tears streamed down her cheeks and her laughter changed to a higher key. Briony heard it and couldn't stop.

When Ford's hand hit her cheek she couldn't believe it. The slap echoed in the air, sharp above the sleepy buzz of bees and insects. Slowly she turned her face and looked up at him, her hysterical laughter shut down abruptly, a look of pain in her brimming eyes.

'You hit me,' she whispered, feeling about ten years old.

Ford smoothed back her hair. 'I'm sorry,' he said gruffly and his brushing away of her tears inexplicably brought more. He got up and drew her to her feet, putting his arms about her and holding her quite still until her shaking stopped. Briony rested her head on his shoulder and let the tears dwindle to a sniffle. And at the moment his arms ceased to be a comfort, became disturbing, she stiffened.

In the canopied shade of the fig tree she lifted her face and saw the change in him. He bent and touched his mouth to hers and the familiar tang of him mingled with the earth-smell of the big tree and the scent of fresh-cut grass that she had dreamed about. Maybe this was a dream, too, she thought as she opened her eyes. The kiss had been featherlight enough to be imaginary. But as he put her away abruptly she knew it was real.

The pain in her knee sharpened as he released her and she hastily put her weight on her other leg. It was the plug of the extension lead that she had landed on. The cord of the chainsaw itself dangled impotently from the tree. She looked up to where the machine was lodged in the branch, then met Ford's eyes.

'I want to talk to you,' he said with a trace of grimness, and began to walk, holding her arm. She limped and he stopped.

'Did you hit your leg?'

'My knee. Nothing serious.'

'Shall I carry you?'

Briony's eyes flew to his face. 'No.'

'I've done it before,' he murmured and a faint smile

curved his mouth as she stirred restlessly beneath his hands.

'I can walk thank you.' But he supported her along the drive, past the pool to the annexe outside her caravan. When she slid into a patio chair she missed the solid warmth of his arm about her waist. Then he sat down near her and her confusion grew with the silence and his steady, thoughtful watching.

'I've fixed the fence,' she blurted out at last, 'And the cobwebs are all cleared now. If you'd arrived later the tree would be trimmed too.'

'If I'd arrived later your very decorative body might be lying on my aunt's front lawn.' His brows drew together and she hardly heard his next words. 'I'd never forgive myself if you'd been injured because of what I said.'

Briony straightened in her chair as his gaze roved her face and shoulders.

'I didn't think for one moment that you would attempt those jobs and frankly I don't expect you to do them.'

Her hazel eyes widened in indignation. 'That wasn't the impression you gave me, Mr Barron. In fact I recall that you considered me a luxury because I wasn't doing everything that the famous Harry did. Well—you just tell me what else he did and I'll do it too. When I take on a job, Mr Barron, I do it all the way, so don't imagine that because helpful Harry was a man that he was any more useful than I am!' She stopped finally, halted by the amusement on Ford's face.

'Harry's reputation I take it, is a little hard to live up to?'

Briony regarded his softened expression with surprise. 'To tell the truth, I'm not wild about Harry.'

He laughed and the sound was rich and deep as it rang out across the pool. Just as quickly his face sobered again. 'My aunt likes you. She seems perfectly happy with your handling of light duties. Let's leave it at that shall we?'

'And your offer of "sideways promotion"?' she asked, unable to forget that hurtful scene. Ford frowned, looked down at his hands.

'An error of judgment—due to overwork and one too many scotches. I apologise. You may not entirely suit this job but I can't deny you're making an effort. You'd better work to Amy's brief in future.'

Briony saw what it was of course. He was still a cynic where she was concerned but he didn't want her possible injuries on his conscience.

'But you intend to watch me like a hawk nevertheless.'

He was silent for a moment, eyes running over her from her tangled, dark hair falling from its pins, to her slim ankles bared between her sneakers and her jeans.

'Yes,' he said at last and stood up. 'I think you bear watching, Briony Wilde.'

'What about the chainsaw? It's jammed in the tree,' she reminded him stiffly.

'I'll attend to that.' He didn't move. Amy Gordon's canary started to sing in his leafy Eden. The notes struck purely into the sleepy buzz of the day.

'Shall I pass a message to Mrs Gordon?' she asked, flushing under his steady scrutiny.

'Message?'

'Didn't you call to see her?'

This time he turned to go. 'No.'

She was still trying to figure out which question he was answering when she went inside the van. There was a burgeoning bruise on her knee she found, but already the pain was easing and she could put her weight on it. At the mirror she ran a brush through her hair and looked at her smudged, confused face. Was she imagining it or had that accident been a step forward?

A few days later a team of professional tree loppers turned up and trimmed the fig.

'Stanford arranged it,' Amy Gordon said. 'He'd noticed it threatening the guttering.'

Looking at the chastened tree Briony nodded. The fig was rather pathetic with its outstretched, amputated limbs.

'Mrs Pratt tells me that you attempted the job, Briony.'

She flushed. Which attempt did she see, she

wondered. 'Oh yes. I wasn't going to mention it. Mr Barron seemed to think I couldn't handle the chainsaw.'

'Oh, my dear, I should think not. Anyway,' she nodded, 'it was very thoughtful of him.'

Briony couldn't decide if it was thoughtfulness that had prompted him or fear that another attempt by her might render him liable for her broken neck. He had certainly seemed genuinely afraid for her safety at the time. Every time she thought of it she shuddered. When the branch had shot upwards, the saw had angled across her still whirring. Only sheer stubbornness had made her do it. With her head for heights she was a fool to have even tried. Maybe, she admitted to herself, she was an idiot to stay here at all . . . but at least she must make an effort not to compound her foolishness by falling into Ford Barron's arms again. That could spell disaster for her in quite another way. In future she must resist the urge to answer him back, to prolong their conversations. Somehow she had to keep away from him. It seemed more imperative now that his attitude appeared to have softened to her.

But, she discovered, Ford Barron was not the only one who could threaten her peaceful existence. Margot Drewett called again and this time she brought her two adolescent sons cast, as Briony found out, in the same mould. She saw the boys watching her, no doubt intrigued by the novelty of a girl gardener, and when their mother went inside with Amy Gordon they came over to where she was working on a thorny, overgrown shrub.

'You're a bit of a change from Harry,' the eldest told her with a rather explicit inspection of her figure. 'I'm Gary Drewett and this is my brother Terry.'

She smiled and continued clipping. 'Hello,' she said casually. They hung about, nudging and winking at each other, making suggestions about the job she was doing in the patronising manner of their mother. Gradually the suggestions altered in tone.

'You've done a lovely job on the front garden beds,' Gary leered as she wouldn't have believed a sixteen-year-old could. 'Why don't you come over to my place

one day, Briony? I've got a bed there that could do with
a bit of attention.' His brother gave a high pitched
giggle and Gary stuck his hands in his pockets and
ogled her. What spoiled brats they were she thought,
more irritated than angry.

'Run away, boys,' she said mildly considering their
rudeness and Gary turned puce. 'And the name's Miss
Wilde.'

'You can't tell me to run away.'

'Go away now and I'll pretend I didn't hear your
innuendo, Gary. This time I'll put it down to childish
ignorance.'

They stood there a moment but Briony's eyes flashed
in real, full-blooded anger and they went, stumbling
through the thorny scrub offcuts.

'You'll be sorry,' Gary shouted as they went inside.

Fifteen minutes later Margot Drewett's piercing voice
hailed her as she wheeled the barrow of cuttings to the
compost heap. Briony's heart sank as the woman came
regally past the pool to her, followed by a remonstrating
Mrs Gordon and the two grinning boys.

'My son tells me you had the audacity to tell them to
run away.'

'That's right, Mrs Drewett.' The prompt admission
made the woman's pale eyes blink.

'How dare you? Just remember that you're the hired
help and have no jurisdiction whatsoever over family
members.'

Mrs Gordon cast what seemed to be an apologetic
glance at Briony as Margot went on to deplore the lack
of deference to her ewe-lambs and to demand an
apology. Briony hesitated, looked at her employer then
at the two boys. Well behind both their mother and
great-aunt they were smug in their immunity.

'On the contrary, Mrs Drewett. I want an apology
and I'll tell you why.'

Briony was never sure if it was Mrs Gordon's support
for her or her sons' humiliation that suffused Margot's
face with rage.

'You can apologise to Briony right now, both of
you,' Amy Gordon said with a hint of steel in her voice.

'And to me. Briony is a friend as well as an employee and I will not tolerate such rudeness to her.'

Margot wouldn't forgive her easily for this, Briony thought, and neither would the boys who made their ungracious apologies and left sullenly.

'Growing up like conceited young savages,' Mrs Gordon frowned when they'd gone.

'I'm sorry about that Mrs Gordon. . . .'

The old lady waved a hand. 'Don't apologise, girl, and call me Amy for goodness sake—all this Mrs Gordon is such a mouthful. Margot's to blame. Not enough discipline and precious few principles.' Her shrewd eyes noted the troubled look on Briony's face. 'Did you think you might put your job in jeopardy by standing up for yourself?'

She nodded.

'That's what I mean. Principles. I knew I was right about you. Backbone,' she said in explanation. 'Too many young people nowadays have nothing but wishbone. You're a lot like Susan.'

It wasn't until days later that Briony found out who Susan was. Amy picked up a photograph from the pianola and showed her.

'My daughter Susan. She was a little older than you when she died. A terrible blow to Robert and I . . . he died five years later. . . .'

'Amy, I'm so sorry——'

'No need, my dear. We had our years together, nothing can change that. In lots of ways I'm luckier than George. He and his wife had no children and she died young. Poor George—so long alone. He was nearly as heartbroken as we were when Susan died in an accident.'

Briony didn't know what to say.

'You're a lot like her, my dear,' Amy went on briskly and returned the photograph of the smiling girl to its place. 'George and I have often commented on it.'

And that explained in part the incredible kindness of the two and maybe why she'd been given the chance at the job. Briony did not know whether to be happy or sad that she resembled a happy, smiling girl who had died an untimely death. But one thing was certain. She wouldn't rely upon the likeness to earn her keep. Briony threw herself into her work, blistering her hands, sustaining scratches, more wasp stings and more than her share of bruises as she wielded unfamiliar tools and tended the garden. And though Amy alternately protested and praised, she also sustained criticism from Ford. There was less bite in it since she had shown herself willing to risk life and limb, but it irritated her nevertheless.

'The fence bolts could be a little tighter, Briony,' he remarked one day when he arrived in a four-wheel-drive vehicle. He was wearing riding clothes and there was an oaty, apply smell about him as if he had been on horseback. Briony looked quickly back to the last of her rose pruning and her heart skipped into a quick rhythm.

'They're as tight as I can make them, Mr Barron,' she said. This time she wouldn't get into one of those crazy conversations with him.

'Not tight enough—but not bad for a guitarist I suppose,' he said and she flashed a look at him, saw the amusement in those blue eyes and said nothing. He was baiting her. 'And did you notice that this post has begun to split?' he went on. She went to look at it.

'No I hadn't. You haven't been using that hammer again have you, Mr Barron?' she couldn't resist saying and to her surprise he laughed.

'Touché.' Small lines crinkled at the corners of his eyes, 'I was rather heavy-handed wasn't I?'

'With the hammer do you mean?' she asked with gentle sarcasm.

He acknowledged the thrust with a rueful downpull of his mouth and went into the house. Before he left again, he fetched a spanner from the tool shed and tightened all the fence bolts she had installed.

'Do you know what to do about that timber split?' he enquired, indicating the fence post.

'Of course,' she said quickly. 'It will have to be filled. And then—um——'

He tossed the spanner down on the grass and put his

❧ IT'S A ❧
HARLEQUIN HONEYMOON
A SWEETHEART
OF A FREE OFFER!

FOUR NEW "HARLEQUIN ROMANCES"—FREE!

Take a "Harlequin Honeymoon" with four exciting romances—yours FREE from Harlequin Reader Service. Each of these hot-off-the-presses novels brings you all the passion and tenderness of today's greatest love stories… your free passports to bright new worlds of love and foreign adventure!

But wait…there's <u>even more</u> to this great offer!

SPECIAL EXTRAS—FREE!

You'll get our free monthly newsletter, packed with news on your favorite writers, upcoming books, and more. Four times a year, you'll receive our members' magazine, Harlequin Romance Digest! <u>Best of all,</u> <u>you'll periodically receive our special-edition "Harlequin Bestsellers," yours to preview for ten days without charge</u>!

MONEY-SAVING HOME DELIVERY!

Join Harlequin Reader Service and enjoy the <u>convenience</u> of previewing six new books every month, delivered right to your home. Each book is yours for only $1.50— <u>25¢ less per book</u> than what you pay in stores! Great savings plus total convenience add up to a sweetheart of a deal for <u>you</u>!

START YOUR HARLEQUIN HONEYMOON TODAY— JUST COMPLETE, DETACH & MAIL YOUR FREE OFFER CARD!

HARLEQUIN READER SERVICE "NO-RISK" GUARANTEE

- There's no obligation to buy—and the free books and gifts remain yours to keep.
- You pay the lowest price possible and receive books before they appear in stores.
- You may end your subscription anytime—just write and let us know.

HARLEQUIN READER SERVICE

❧ FREE OFFER CARD ❧

PLACE HEART STICKER HERE

4 FREE BOOKS

PLUS AN EXTRA BONUS "MYSTERY GIFT"!

FREE HOME DELIVERY

☐ **YES!** Please send me my four HARLEQUIN ROMANCES® books, <u>free</u>, along with my <u>free Mystery Gift</u>! Then send me six new HARLEQUIN ROMANCES books every month, as they come off the presses, and bill me at just $1.50 per book (25¢ less than retail), with no extra charges for shipping and handling. If I am not completely satisfied, I may return a shipment and cancel at any time. <u>The free books and Mystery Gift remain mine to keep!</u>

116 CIR EAXF

FIRST NAME_____ LAST NAME_____
                              (PLEASE PRINT)

ADDRESS_____ APT._____

CITY_____

PROV./STATE_____ POSTAL CODE/ZIP_____

PRINTED IN U.S.A.

hands on his hips, looking down at her where she knelt by the garden bed. 'Maintenance girl—what a joke. I daresay you'll find something about it in that well-thumbed library book on the workbench.'

She coloured but put her chin up. 'Probably. I'm not ashamed to admit that I have to seek expert advice to do the job. Your aunt knew that when she hired me.'

'Just so long as you go by the book, Briony.'

That again. 'With you as watchdog, Mr Barron, could I do otherwise?'

'I don't know,' he murmured, then, apropos of nothing, 'How's your knee?'

'Fine. Just bruised.' She warmed a little at the memory of that incident. 'I won't be putting in any outrageous claims for compensation if that's what you're thinking.'

'Well do you know, I hadn't considered that——' he told her. 'All this fresh air must be going to my head.'

'Careful, Mr Barron. You might end up trusting me yet.' Glancing up she found him watching with the oddest expression.

'I might at that,' he said to her astonishment. 'It would simplify things.'

CHAPTER SIX

AND just what that meant she wasn't certain. Trying to establish where she stood with Ford Barron wasn't easy. His holiday must be making him more agreeable though, she allowed. The frown had lifted from his brow—he seemed to have shed some of his cynicism. It should be a relief, but the idea of a relaxed, teasing Ford Barron dropping by bothered her almost as much as the previous situation.

But at least he confined his visits to the daytime. At night he must have other things to occupy him for she never heard his voice up at the house with Amy. Very likely Elizabeth Campbell reaped the benefits of his free nights, she reflected as she sat on the van steps and plucked her guitar one evening. Amy had gone to a dinner and a few pleasant hours stretched ahead until she had to bring her back.

The night was mild, a hint of spring drawing nearer and only the flutter of moths about the annexe light, the croak of a frog and the last evening song of Amy's canary could be heard. The sky was indigo, glittering with stars that were caught a second time in the silvered water of the pool. Enchanted with the perfect blend of the night's sight and sound, Briony played a delicate picking pattern and sang 'Plaisir d'amour'. The haunting melody melded with the evening's flawlessness. As the last notes hung on the air, a shoe scuffed on the flagstones. As the last note hummed in the guitar beneath her fingers, Briony knew who it was.

Ford Barron strolled into the pale gold pool of light and her heart began performing its calypso rhythm again.

'You play beautifully.' He was looking her over as she stood, remembering perhaps a different image—boots and a low-slung electric guitar.

'Thanks.'

'You have a delightful voice.' He smiled at her startled expression. 'Your performance with the band led me to believe you could only strum a few chords and look beautiful.'

Look beautiful? With her kohl-rimmed, glitter-sprinkled eyes and crimped hair? He must be joking.

'Strum a few chords?' she repeated, picking up the least personal of his remarks. 'Playing pop music requires a bit more than that, Mr Barron.'

'Ford. Call me Ford. And I don't believe your musical ability was seriously extended by that stuff you were playing at the Gala.'

'I could say you're wrong but you don't believe anything much I say do you, Mr Barron?'

'With you, Briony, I find I'm—selective.' He smiled and, guitar in hand she moved quickly aside to let him in as he mounted the steps with the clear intention of entering. A little indignant she followed him in and put her guitar away.

'Won't you come in, Mr Barron?' she asked with heavy sarcasm and her pulses hammered at the sight of this tall figure in the close confinement of the van. She was reminded of that first time he'd marched her here and said those harsh words. Tonight though he didn't look as if harsh words could pass his lips—and that was just as disquieting.

Unperturbed, he sat down at the tiny dining table. 'Thank you, Briony.'

'Would you like some coffee?'

While she boiled the water and spooned instant powder into the cups Briony saw him look around the van as he had done the last time. The plant in its cane planter held his attention for a few moments but he didn't comment on the change except to say: 'You must be whispering sweet nothings to it—it looks healthy even in its less exotic holder.'

Amy must have told him that she talked to her plant which must make her sound a bit peculiar—but no more peculiar than his aunt.

'I simply say pleasant things to it,' she told him, 'Maybe I should put it outside while you're here.'

'Why—do you intend to say something unpleasant.'

She gave him a level look. 'No.'

'But you think I will?'

'Don't you always?'

'I started off with a compliment tonight.'

'Yes—why?'

'So suspicious, Briony. It was true, that's why.'

She laughed as she poured boiling water into the cups. 'Me—suspicious—that's a laugh. You're the most suspecting person I know.' As she turned to put the cups down he seemed to be considering that.

'Maybe,' he admitted and smiled at her exaggerated reaction to his honesty. 'When you fell at my feet that first time I suspected you were pretending—feinting not fainting.'

'What?' Briony was startled and wondered how long it had taken him to find out it was for real. 'Did you catch me?'

He shook his head. 'Afraid not. I picked you up off the ground. You didn't weigh much.'

'I weigh more now.'

'So I noticed the next time you fell—out of the tree.' He flexed his shoulders. 'I was sore for days.'

'If you hadn't glared at me I wouldn't have lost my footing,' she retorted. 'I could have done the job you know.'

Ford stopped his coffee halfway to his mouth. 'You haven't attempted to use that chainsaw again, have you?'

She reached into a cupboard and drew out a tin of biscuits. As she put them on the table he took her wrist.

'Have you?' he insisted.

'No, of course not.' He looked down at her hand still held in his grasp. One thumb moved over the slender breadth of her wrist to her palm. 'Why on earth did Amy take you on,' he murmured. 'Even when you're healthy you have a fragile look.'

'You sound just like my brother. He thought I was a fool to apply for the job on the grounds that I wasn't built for the life.'

With a half smile Ford let her hand go. He took a

biscuit from the tin and inspected it. 'In that case I shall try not to mention your fragility and unsuitability again.'

She stared.

'I don't want to sound like your brother.' Their eyes held across the tiny table. 'I don't think I want that at all.'

There was a silence before he bit into the cookie.

'Where did these come from?' he enquired, munching.

'I baked them,' she said, hoping her face wasn't as pink as it felt. Brother, she thought. There was precious little chance of her confusing him with a brother and he knew it.

'They're good.'

'I know. Have another.'

'I was hoping you'd say that.' He eyed her as he helped himself to another. 'I hear you've had words with Margot?'

Hot coffee burned her throat as she gulped. 'You could say that. I—demanded an apology because her son made certain suggestions that I didn't care for.'

'Did he indeed? I wondered why she didn't go into detail.' His gaze wandered over her shining dark hair which was loose about her shoulders, over the glowing skin and tawny hazel eyes with their long lashes. 'He always was an abominable kid, but I didn't suspect he would show such taste.'

'Mr Barron—I'm not accustomed to being propositioned by grotty sixteen-year-olds. True,' she said, heavily sarcastic, 'it's not the first tasteless one I've been offered lately, but the familiarity of the situation makes it no easier. I don't think it's a matter for joking.'

He was caught with his hand in the biscuit barrel yet again. Still keyed up from her outburst, Briony saw the humorous aspects of a suddenly grim-faced Ford reaching for a cookie.

'My—proposition as you call it—was entirely different,' he grated. 'Made in unfortunate circumstances and without proper consideration. And I did apologise.'

Briony was sorry she had brought the subject up at

all. Just the memory of his suggestion brought the heat rushing to her face. 'Yes, you did. I shouldn't have mentioned it again,' she admitted.

Ford relaxed again. 'That's not to say of course, that certain parts of it weren't a good idea.'

'I don't know what you mean.' She avoided his eye.

'Yes I think you do. But I have learned not to make the same mistake twice.'

'Oh good,' she said, cheeks flaming now, 'does that mean you won't offer me a nice little pied à terre in town again?'

'Why—do you fancy one now?' he asked with exaggerated interest.

'No,' she almost shouted. 'I don't want anything from you—or from anyone else for that matter.'

'You're a woman—and women always want something. I've yet to discover just what it is you're after.' He looked disconcertingly at her and her head whirled at yet another change of mood. He was the most bewildering man. Within the space of a few minutes he had been charming, disarming, accusatory.

'Rest easy, Mr Barron—I've heard all about the women who chase you and your wealth. Whatever I'm after—it's not you.'

He stopped chewing a moment then swallowed.

'I'm really very wealthy,' he said mildly.

Briony shrugged.

'Some would say "filthy rich" I suppose,' he went on.

She half smiled at his mock-thoughtful air. 'So?'

'Loaded.' He nodded. 'Yes, that's the term. I'm loaded.'

'Oh, in that case—loaded—that's different.' She leaned forward confidentially, 'Could I refer you to a friend of mine? I'd hate to waste a perfectly good millionaire.'

His laughter burst out, loud in the confined space. What a difference it made she thought, stripping away the remnants of tension and the years from his face making him boyish and human and more dangerous than ever.

'Quick with the repartee—are you sure you weren't

born within sound of Bow bells? Was that Cockney accent a sometime inheritance from a parent perhaps?'

'No, my parents were both Australian. I was born in . . .' she stopped suddenly realising she'd used the past tense about her parents, '. . . a very ordinary town.'

'But you're not an ordinary girl,' he murmured, 'Just what kind of a girl are you, Briony?'

'I thought you had that all figured out,' she said sharply. 'Your cousins seem to have come to the same conclusion.'

'That's doubtful. My conclusions are far from complete. But Margot was certainly fairly definite about hers. She was beside herself.' Complacently he finished his third biscuit and brushed crumbs from his corduroy jacket. In a cream silky shirt he seemed browner than ever and the russet coloured cut velvet accentuated the breadth of his shoulders. Fascinated, Briony found herself looking at the way his dark hair touched the collar of his jacket and was brushed back from his forehead with the suggestion of a wave. 'You had every right to be annoyed. Actually you saved me a job. That boy needed a jolt,' he said.

Briony's mouth dropped open in mock amazement. 'Please, Mr Barron. This amiability is too much. Do give me a severe talking to—a few warnings. Frown down your arrogant nose at me and put me at ease again.'

'Is that how I strike you—as arrogant?'

'Yes. And superior and autocratic—and prejudiced and inflexible.' She grinned at him. 'Other than that you're not too bad.'

'I must have some saving qualities?'

'Yes,' she sighed. 'I suppose you must.'

Ford laughed and stayed on for another cup of coffee and gently probed for details of her background. And now that she had the chance to tell him she was evasive. Perhaps it was her stubborn streak. And maybe it was sheer instinct, guarding her from what could be the start of another, permanent fall at his feet.

Eventually he got up to leave and she went out into the annexe with him.

'Your aunt is at a dinner party.'

'I didn't come to see Amy.'

'Oh.' She waved away a moth that had blundered from the van's light, then shivered a little in the cooling evening air.

'You're cold?'

'Yes——' she began and stammered, '——no,' as he dropped his arm about her shoulders and walked with her towards the pool's deep turquoise, glowing in the light that shone beside it.

'I'm having a party next weekend while Amy is away. Will you come?' he asked.

Her heart began a reggae strut rhythm. A party? Amy would be staying the weekend with an old school friend. Was that in some way connected with the invitation?

'So that you can keep me under surveillance, Mr Barron?' she said lightly. Around her his arm tensed, pulling her close beside him. When he stopped and slipped both arms about her, Briony was nearly deafened by her pulsebeat.

'You could call it that. I feel I don't want you out of my sight,' he murmured. 'Will you come?'

'I don't think——'

'Please,' he said and the single word brought her head up in surprise. 'It could be my last party. The following day I jump again.'

'It won't be your last,' she pulled slightly against his restraining arms, 'you aren't the destructible type—not even vulnerable.'

'Now there, Briony Wilde, you are way out of tune. I'm a damned sight more vulnerable than I want to be. . . .' The marbled reflections of the pool flickered across his cheek then were gone as abruptly he pulled her close.

It was different, Briony knew at once as his mouth took hers. The potent chemistry had another ingredient and she tried to identify it, but her senses beguiled her away from anything so mundane as thought. Ford's hands were spread warmly across her back, pressing her close so that the ridged velvet texture of his jacket and the silky feel of his shirt were beneath her fingertips. Briony spun into a star-spangled space that began and ended with Ford's touch. Her hands sought the solidity of his shoulders, slipped over them to clasp about his neck where the hair touched his collar, and as her lips opened to his, the moist, warm intimacy of his invasion drew a small sound from her. Ford drew back, his breathing quick and warm on her still parted mouth. His arms were loose about her and now that she could have pulled away she did not. But when he bent his head to kiss her again she turned her head, before she lost it completely.

'Don't, Ford, please——'

'Say you'll come next Saturday then,' he whispered.

'I'm your aunt's gardener—I wouldn't fit in——' His head descended. 'And your aunt might not like me to——' Closer. 'It wouldn't be——' Closer still. 'All right—yes. I'll come to your party.'

Almost against her lips he said: 'Pick you up at seven.'

She nodded.

'Will you stay overnight?' At her stiffening, he smiled. 'There'll be others staying over too, Briony. I told you I don't make the same mistake twice.'

'I'd rather come home thank you,' she said primly. Had there been 'others staying over' that first time he'd invited her to stay?

'Then I'll bring you back home.' His arms slid from her waist and the cool night air rushed in to chill her where his warmth had been. 'Goodnight, Briony.'

'Goodnight, Ford.'

He whistled as he walked around the pool and then along the leafy drive. It was a tuneful rendition of 'Plaisir d'amour'. At last the sound stopped and the roar of an engine burst on the night's silence then it too was gone.

Another dream? Briony thought, and stood there by the shimmering water looking up at a skyful of stars. It was the setting for romance, for dreaming. A quiet 'plop' brought her gaze downwards again and she searched the pool surface for its source. A laugh broke from her as she saw the tiny green frog swimming close to the side. It was the reversal of the fairy-tale she saw—an omen perhaps.

She kissed the prince and was left with a frog. She must remember that.

'Is something bothering you, Briony?' Amy asked on the way home from her dinner party.

'Well yes—your nephew called. He—invited me to a party while you're away next week. Would it be all right for me to go, do you think?'

Amy turned a curious look on her. 'A party? Hmmm.' She paused. 'Of course it's all right my dear. Why wouldn't it be?'

'I'm sure gardeners don't usually mix socially with their employer's family.'

The old lady chuckled. 'Well I have to say that poor old Harry never got invited to one of Stanford's gatherings. Then again—Harry didn't have your looks or figure.'

'Ah but Harry could handle a chainsaw, Harry could mend fences in a flesh, Harry could lift the engine from the car with one hand tied behind his back,' Briony said tongue in cheek.

Laughing, Amy touched her arm affectionately. 'Yes, Harry was a dear, useful fellow but I have to confess that he had no sense of humour.'

'Aha,' Briony grinned. 'At last something that Helpful Harry didn't have. Wait till I tell Ford——'

She stopped abruptly, embarrassed at the intimate sound of that. Amy pursed her lips a little and looked thoughtful.

'You're a very pretty girl, Briony, and a sensible one. Stanford is—how can I say this—in his quiet way he has something of a reputation.' She hesitated. 'I wouldn't like you to become one of his casualties my dear.'

'There's no fear of that.' No? If she was honest she would admit she was already in danger. But if she remembered the gulf that separated herself and Ford surely she would not become a 'casualty'. And one

reckless part of her wanted to take the chance—to peek
into his life—and then. . . .

Before Briony waved her off on the train on Friday,
Amy pressed a small box into her hand.

'Just a trinket that might look good with that swish
dress of yours,' she said carelessly. Amy had asked if
she had anything to wear to Ford's party—a fair
enough question considering she had only seen her odd-
job girl wearing jeans and overalls—and duly been
shown the green dress. Her faded eyes had studied it
with approval. 'Lovely, my dear.' Then in seeming
irrelevance, 'Did you leave a boyfriend behind in the
city, Briony?'

'Only one I wanted to leave behind.'

'Mmm. Just be—careful with my nephew won't you?'

'Of course. I promise not to harm a hair on his head,'
she said gravely.

Amy chuckled and patted her on the shoulder. 'You
know what I'm getting at, Briony. That sense of
humour won't always come to your rescue.'

With reminders to feed Victor, water the sunroom
plants and to be sure and take time off, Amy
relinquished all the keys and cheerfully sat back in her
train seat, an Agatha Christie already open and her
reading glasses perched on her nose.

The 'trinket' turned out to be a magnificent simple
gold chain with a green stone. Briony held it up to the
light. Was it an emerald, or just glass? She couldn't tell
but decided it was unlikely to be the real thing if Amy
loaned it so casually. At any rate it looked fantastic
against the green dress.

By lunch time on Saturday Briony looked back with
satisfaction on her achievements. The lawn was smooth,
the pool crystal clear and the car clean. She went into
the house to feed the canary and water the plants, and
even though Amy had asked her to do so, she felt
uneasy about it. Victor chirruped and trilled as she
carefully checked that all the windows and doors were
locked. Then she decided to take the canary to the van
with her, so that she wouldn't have to open the house
up again. The bird lapsed into silence for a time when

she placed his cage on the table in the annexe but by the time she returned from the shower, her long hair dripping, the sweet notes of his singing welcomed her.

As the afternoon galloped towards evening, she became restless with anticipation and anxiety. She had only to think of Ford to be completely confused. As she sat in the sun drying her hair and painting her fingernails, it was almost impossible to think of anything else.

'Bother,' she exclaimed as her unsteady hand dropped a blob of nail polish on her skin. She uncapped the remover and wiped the coral stain away. It wasn't as if attending a party was anything new for her after all, she remonstrated with herself. Plenty of attractive men had taken her out in the past—attractive men. But she sighed—not in Ford Barron's class. And none of them had ever caused the slightest smudge in her nail polish.

George turned up while she sat lazily brushing her almost dry hair. He sniffed the sharp smell of acetate polish remover and made a face.

'And you women have the nerve to complain about a pipe.' He reached for his pipe as he said it and raised an eyebrow in query.

'Go right ahead, George,' she grinned and he took out his tobacco pouch and sat down to the pleasant task of lighting up.

'Now that's better than the smell of that stuff you've got there, isn't it?' he asked when he took his first puff.

'Much better. And awfully macho.'

He chortled and drew complacently on the pipe stem, regarding her through the fine veil of smoke. 'Going to Ford's party tonight, Amy tells me.'

'That's right.'

'Ford's quite a catch,' he murmured and Briony stiffened. 'Don't get on your high horse,' he said, 'I just mean that he's used to females running after him and—you might be a bit of a novelty.'

'Are you warning me not to let Ford turn my head, George?'

'Your head's a bit firmer screwed on than that.

There's no problem so long as it's only your head that's involved.'

A novelty, Briony thought and mentally squirmed at the idea.

'I know I'm not Ford's kind of girl. Elizabeth Campbell is.'

The pipe pointed upwards. 'How do you know about Elizabeth?'

'Oh——' she could hardly confess that she'd met her at Ford's house after having fainted at his feet as a finale to the Gala disaster. 'I believe Amy or someone mentioned her.'

'Well—Elizabeth's been keen on Ford for a while. Her family and his have been friends for years and the two mothers always had hopes of a marriage.' He lapsed into silence, contentedly smoking.

'And——' she prompted. 'Will there be one?'

'Don't think so. Ford's Mum gave up on it a few years back and went off to Italy with Ted—that's his Dad. Ford used to see a lot of Elizabeth on and off and she hasn't given up. She's smart enough to back off for a while but she's never far away. I think she'd like to be mistress of Abingdon and play hostess in Ford's Sydney place.'

'She'd be good at it,' Briony conceded and her spirits sank a little.

'But not good for him necessarily. He's a bit lukewarm about Elizabeth these days. Lukewarm about a lot of things. I reckon that's why he started up with this parachuting business again. Jaded.'

He looked meaningfully at Briony and she managed a laugh. 'Then I'd better be very dull and uninteresting. I wouldn't want to catch the eye of a jaded executive.'

George looked at her shining hair, the slim curves of her face and body. 'Better put a sack over your head then.'

'George—is that a compliment?'

He nodded. 'Never was much at expressing myself.' He got up to go. 'Enjoy yourself. Phone me if you need anything while Amy's away. Oh, and——' he turned back, 'a few of those carnation plants might see another season if you give them a trimming. Keep the cuttings—but I expect you know that.'

He ambled off and Briony wondered if her feckless brother had really known about carnations or if it was a lucky guess.

Long before seven she was ready, her hair swept up into a knot, make-up applied and Amy's pendant hanging in the deep neckline of the green dress. With the new golden tan of her outdoors life, the fabric glowed brilliantly, lending greenish tones to her hazel eyes and its subtle promise realised as it skimmed and clung and swirled over the curves of her body. A smile of satisfaction lifted her glossed mouth. At last Ford would see the real Briony Wilde. Not a comic strip waif with glitter-fringed eyes, or a jeans-and-T-shirt earth girl covered with grime. Perfume and long-necked sophistication—it made a change from overalls. 'The real me,' she said and curtsied to her own reflection.

Victor trilled a couple of times when she put him inside out of range of cats and dogs, but fell silent as she dropped a cloth over his cage. With a totally unsuitable but warm jacket over her arm and Amy's house keys carefully stowed in her clutch bag, she nervously went outside. The narrow heels of her patent sandals clicked on the van steps and she locked the door. Already the van light was surrounded by a fleet of fluttering moths.

Slowly, she walked around the cabana, past its single light and waited by one of the pool's nymph statues. A breeze rippled the water and shushed through the leaves of the potted palms and rattled the pods on the cassia tree that grew down by the back boundary. The moon was a sliver of light sailing behind a tracery of cloud and a few stars sprinkled the pool's surface. Somewhere the frog croaked and almost at once came the crisp sound of footsteps on the flagstones.

Ford's tall image shimmered in the water and Briony looked up to see the real man standing on the other side of the aqua expanse. Though his face was shadowed, she saw the gleam of his eyes as they moved over her. The moon tacked from beneath a sail of cloud and silvered the outline of his dark head as he came around the curved pool's edge to her. He stopped a few feet from her, saying nothing but his eyes eloquent as they roved this new image. Like an adolescent she waited for some sweet word of admiration then forced back the disappointment when he merely took the coat from her arm and slung it over his. When he took her hands in his though her heart began its frivolous rhythm.

'You're very prompt,' he said at last. 'I expected to wait at least ten minutes.'

'I always try to do the unexpected,' she told him flippantly.

'So I've noticed. But I'm glad you didn't feel the need to be too unexpected tonight.' He looked meaningfully at her suitable dress and the classic hair style.

'Well I did toy with the idea of boots and sequins,' she joked though there was a hint of asperity in her tone, 'but it was rather cool this evening.'

What had he imagined? That she would be dressed in some outlandish gear—be embarrassingly unsuitable to present to his guests?

'That outfit had its merits . . . but this one is beyond reproach.' He sounded amused and she bit back her retort as she realised he was teasing.

They traversed the pool and as they drew level with the house he stopped and held out his hand. 'Have you got Amy's keys. I'd better check that everything's locked.'

She was on the defensive immediately. 'There's no need for that. I've already checked the windows and doors.'

'I meant from inside.'

'I've done that.'

'I see.' She flushed under his scrutiny, annoyed at the hint of remaining distrust. All his initial warnings came back to her.

'Yes I went in to feed the canary and water the plants and locked up at the same time. And I resisted the awful temptation to leave a window open for a spot of burglary by one of my "undesirable" friends.'

He was silent, serious. 'All right. Let's leave it at

that,' he said at length, but instead of moving on he waited there, hands shoved into the pockets of the fine wool battle jacket he wore.

'Tell me,' he said and she tensed, 'Where did you go that night you ran away from me?'

'What does it matter?' she prevaricated. Not for worlds would she admit to sleeping on the Ladies' Room bench. And why did he ask that question now?

'You turned up here the next morning for an interview. Early the next morning. You didn't stay at the hotel. Who put you up for the night—Neil?'

'Neil?' she echoed stupidly, scarcely recognising the name. 'The man who came into your study with Elizabeth Campbell?'

'Her cousin. Yes.'

'Of course not. I don't even know him.'

'Would that matter?' he asked and she stepped back as if he had struck her.

'I don't believe I want to come to your party after all, Mr Barron,' she said in a stiff voice and began to walk away. He caught her by the shoulders and whirled her back to face him.

'I'm sorry. That was a stupid thing to say,' he grated. 'Forget what I said.'

'Just what is it all about?' she demanded, her anger rising.

'Forget it,' he said again, 'Neil said something that made me think maybe he'd followed up on that offer he made you in my study.'

'Well he didn't.' She raised her chin at the look in his eyes. 'Just as I didn't follow up on your offer. And I'm not saying where I stayed. Go to your party, Mr Barron, and I'll stay home. You wouldn't want an undesirable like me around.'

Ford bent his head to look into her stormy face. 'That's just the trouble, Briony,' he muttered. 'You're anything but undesirable.'

'That wasn't what I——' she gasped as his fingers moved caressingly on her arms, levered her close. And in spite of her anger, when he lifted a hand to lightly trace the shape of her face in the moonlight, she abandoned her attempt to move away.

'And I definitely want you around,' he murmured before he dropped a kiss, light as a feather on her lips. Had he kissed her more deeply she might have run. But the gentle salute struck just the right note of persuasion and apology and when he began to walk with her along the drive she made no demur. As he saw her into the car, she was reminded of all the warnings she'd received about this man. Amy, George, she herself had issued cautions against losing her head. Firmly, she ran through them all again.

The car purred along the narrow road and Ford drove out that awkward scene with his casual talk about the guests invited. It was part pleasure, part duty he told her. More than half those invited had been involved in running the Gala fête and this was a belated thank you to them. Briony's hands fidgeted on her bag. As a member of Silverhero, she was hardly likely to be popular with them. She said as much to Ford who glanced quickly at her.

'I'm afraid I didn't think about that,' he admitted with faint surprise. 'It was a purely selfish move to want you there.'

And that was enough to send her spirits soaring. All those warnings chattered away in the back of her mind and she stopped listening to them. But it occurred to her that her hopes rose and fell as regularly as the horses on the carousel at the Gala. Around in circles and up and down. Knowing Ford had spoiled her sense of direction.

CHAPTER SEVEN

Two other cars were parked in his drive. Long, expensive vehicles which gave a fair indication as to the financial worth of his friends.

'Aren't you a little late to greet your guests?'

'Not at all. Those cars belong to the friends who arrived earlier today—they'll be staying over tonight.' He slanted a look at Briony as he parked the car. 'You see—it was quite above board.'

Her cheeks warmed. 'But what about the first time you invited me to stay? Who was sleeping over then?'

His door opened and shut and he came around to the passenger side. As she stepped out, he hooked an arm about her waist and grinned. 'Ah—the first time wasn't above board.'

He slammed the door, then pulled her close against his side and laughing, walked her up the broad steps. Briony realised that she might never know what he had intended that night. Ford stopped on the terrace and exclaimed at the sight of a battered station sedan that was parked farther along—an odd contrast to the gleaming imported monsters.

By the time they entered the high-ceilinged reception room and Ford had introduced her to the two couples already there, it was plain that he was looking about for someone. 'Stuart——' he exclaimed as a tall, thin young man dashed in and slapped him on the back. Briony watched curiously as both men talked at once, Ford laughing even as his keen gaze slid over the younger man's thin features. She recognised the same concern that Jeff had sometimes worn for her—and vice versa. So this was Ford's younger brother—who played drums in a band and who brought a look of paternal anxiety to Ford's face.

'Is everything okay?' she heard him ask and the reply came with a cheerful shrug.

'Sure.' Stuart grinned and Briony saw the similarity between the brothers deepen. Except that Stuart looked as if he might smile a great deal more often. 'I know you weren't expecting me until tomorrow, but I was at a loose end and came straight on.' He pulled a face. 'I didn't bank on walking in on one of your parties though, Ford.'

'You'll love it,' his brother smiled. 'I'm entertaining the Silver Spoon committee tonight among others.'

Stuart groaned. 'Margot?'

'Technically speaking I needn't have invited her—she wasn't here for the Gala. Politically—it would have been suicide to leave the secretary off the invitation list.'

'An early night,' Stuart said. 'That's what I need, now I come to think of it.' He looked around and saw Briony. 'On the other hand. . . .' His eyes, less blue and more grey than Ford's, lit up in appreciation, 'One should always make an effort for one's family.'

As Ford made the introductions Briony sensed a change in him. Though he smiled on his brother's enthusiastic greeting to her, his blue eyes cooled a fraction, he drew a cloak of reserve about him.

'Ford—you go right ahead and play host,' Stuart told him as a car purred to a halt outside. 'I'll be glad to look after Briony. As a duty, of course.'

Ford went, taking her coat and bag to an inner room first and Stuart informed her earnestly that he was the family's black sheep. 'You won't mind being seen with me?' he asked and she laughed. Now wasn't the time to tell him, but he had met probably the only other black sheep to turn up here tonight. Ford went past them and spared a glance at their laughter—but strangely there was none in his eyes.

The party was to occupy the long, broad terrace that lay along the back of the house. Briony's only memory of it was a dim lit one as she'd fled through the house to leave by one of the several sliding glass doors that panelled the glass wall. Now she could see that it was luxuriously fitted with a gleaming bar and dotted with chairs and tables, the whole garlanded with lush plants that clustered in corners and hung between the huge white globes that emitted a discreet, encouraging light. A small area was clearly marked as a dance floor and a buffet was set up, the arrangement of foods a magnificent still life on a grand scale. Outside garden lights played over a slate patio and furniture. She had left Ford's coat on one of those chairs.

'So,' Stuart put a drink into her hand, 'you're Ford's lat—I mean, girlfriend.'

'We're just good friends,' she quipped.

'Of course,' he nodded and his grey eyes twinkled at her in an amazing likeness of Amy's. She had seen and not recognised at first, the similarity between the old lady and Ford, but Stuart was more like her.

In jeans and casual shirt, Stuart appeared perfectly at ease, greeting one or two of the elegant crowd and introducing them to Briony. His tall figure lounged beside her and Briony sneaked a look at him over her drink. Apart from a strong nose and attractively wide shoulders, Stuart bore little resemblance to Ford until he smiled. There was less physical substance about him—and a great deal more approachability. Briony was particularly thankful for his presence when Margot and her husband arrived. They greeted Stuart with the patronising affection reserved, Briony imagined, for family black sheep. They both treated Briony to a freezing reception. There was malice and speculation in Margot's eyes and straightforward speculation in her husband's as they took in her vastly changed appearance. For the first time Briony saw how her presence might be misconstrued and she wished she hadn't been so foolish as to accept Ford's invitation. A sudden rush of anger shook the drink in her hand as Margot and Doug drifted away to greet warmly a guest who met their approval. Why on earth had Ford invited her anyway? He hadn't even spoken to her since they arrived. If it hadn't been for Stuart's unexpected arrival, she might have been standing about, a fish out of water, trying to make conversation with strangers.

'Now that,' Stuart said reflectively, 'was a glacial reception even for cool-cousin-Margot. Not like her to look down on a girlfriend of Ford's.'

'I'm not his girlfriend,' she informed him shortly, 'I'm your aunt's gardener.'

Stuart threw back his head and roared. 'And I'm Ringo Starr.'

'It's true. Ask Amy.'

He whistled, eyes round and brows raised. Then he shot a look at Ford who was smiling and listening to one of the guests.

'And Ford invited you to his party——?' he murmured.

'That's right. Though why I can't imagine,' she said abruptly, annoyed at his near desertion of her.

'Hmmm. Well I can think of a couple of reasons,' Stuart said and his glance down at her was warm and admiring.

Ford chose that moment to pause by them. He looked a little stiff as they both turned to him.

'Would you like another drink, Briony?' he asked. He had removed his jacket and his wide-shouldered body was leanly attractive in the wine-coloured shirt that lay open at the neck. She shook her head and Stuart grinned, urged him to circulate.

'I'll be delighted to fetch and carry for Briony,' he declared, a gleam of devilment in his eyes. 'This looks like being one of your better parties, Ford.'

And Ford moved away again. His 'purely selfish move' to have her here seemed a bit of a joke, Briony thought.

'Now tell me,' Stuart said, 'why did Margot freeze you?'

'Oh that,' Briony tried to make light of it, 'it was just er—a disagreement we had about her son.'

'Which one? The abominable Gary or the abominable Terry?'

She admitted it was Gary and gradually related the story.

Stuart whistled. 'Spoiled brat. Serves him right. But just watch your step with those two young thugs. They've been so thoroughly ruined that they can't bear things to go against them.'

'Let's not get melodramatic,' Briony laughed. 'They're just kids after all.'

'Don't say you haven't been warned if you find a spider in your bed—a frog in your gum boots—a dead bat in your wardrobe.'

'Ugh,' she stared at him.

'I speak from experience.' The lugubrious expression that accompanied it made her laugh again. She caught Ford's eye again through the crowd and his unsmiling face dimmed her amusement. The face beside his dimmed it lower again.

It was Elizabeth Campbell's. Next to her was a prosperous-looking man of perhaps forty and behind them were several young people including Neil whom she'd seen last in Ford's study. Oh no, she thought. How could he have invited her here where she would have to meet them again?

'This is going to be quite a night—with cousin Margot outraged at the inclusion of Auntie's gardener—and one who has had the temerity to tick off her darling eldest.' Stuart chortled into his drink and Briony dryly warned him to be ready for even greater entertainment as Elizabeth's eyes lighted on her. So far there was no recognition in them, but she had only to hear the name and she would put two and two together. Margot made her regal way to join Elizabeth and Briony turned away. Damn!

'You might as well be the first to know,' she said to Stuart, as one outcast to another and told him the story of Silverhero and the Gala.

'And the band left without you?'

'Without me.'

'And what happened then?'

Uncomfortably she shifted her weight from one foot to the other. Elizabeth was chatting with Margot. The boy Neil was giving a second look to her and Stuart.

'I—your brother chewed me out and I fainted.'

'And?' The grey eyes regarded her shrewdly, more than ever like Amy's. Inwardly she groaned. What would Amy make of it all—she was bound to hear about it.

'Oh nothing much. He revived me so that my brother could chew me out later.'

Stuart was intrigued. With another glance to where

Ford was aiding the barman to dispense cocktails, Stuart asked, 'What instrument do you play?' and she told him, well aware that he was suppressing the questions he really wanted to ask.

Their conversation became more professional as he told her a little of his own life in the band of which he'd been a member for four years.

'Before that——' he paused and his mobile face became serious, 'I was with another group, but that is a long and sordid story,' he finished lightly and hailed a young couple who had just come in.

He introduced them as Ken Murray and Lila, his wife. Ken was short and wiry and pleasantly ordinary. His wife clung to his arm and in the bright gathering the two seemed a pair of grey doves—quiet, unassuming. So Briony was startled to hear Stuart ask Ken about skydiving. The man's ordinary face grew animated and his wife's hand curled tighter about his arm.

'Yes—I'm still an addict,' he grinned. 'I'm not drinking tonight. Apollo has a practice run tomorrow and I never drink and dive.' Lila smiled wanly at this obviously old joke and Ken looked down at her and patted her hand. 'Did you know Ford's jumping with us again?' he asked Stuart. 'He's filling in for poor old Colin—he's in pretty good shape considering he hasn't jumped for so long. Relative work's hard enough when you're at it consistently.'

'He's a natural,' Stuart nodded. 'Why has he gone back to it now though?'

'The team is the subject of a television documentary. If Ford hadn't been prepared to come back—we might never get to see ourselves on-screen.' He shook his head. 'Poor old Colin couldn't have struck out at a worse time.'

'Relative work—what's that?' Briony asked, wondering what had happened to Colin, but lacking the courage to ask.

'That's what we call the manoeuvres we have to learn to line ourselves up for the formations. Sometimes you need to slow your fall, sometimes speed it up to be in the right place relative to the others.'

'But—don't you just all jump out at the same time?' she said, 'I mean, how can you possibly fall slower than someone else?'

Ford joined them, an eyebrow raised at her question, as if he was surprised to find them talking on the subject.

'The suits help,' Stuart explained. 'They're designed to catch the air—hasn't my big brother told you anything about his daredevil skydiving days?'

She shook her head, conscious of the faint stirring of nerves in her stomach. Her eyes went briefly to Ford and she had a sudden vision of him hurtling through the air towards the ground.

'Why do you do it?' she asked Ken. Lila smiled patiently.

'Good question,' she said to Briony.

'There is no real answer for someone who's never done it,' Ken said to Briony, looking more closely at her since Stuart had bracketed her with Ford. 'The first time you do it I suppose it's a sort of dare with yourself.'

'What is it like?' She stared at Ken, amazed at her need to know. It was suddenly, terribly important that she knew.

'It's—terror, exhilaration—truth I guess. There's only you—but it's a you that you didn't know existed. You're never the same again afterwards. . . .' Embarrassed, Ken glanced at Ford, took a mouthful of his drink and when he looked up the glow had gone from his eyes. He was an ordinary man again.

'Skygods,' Stuart said and grinned at Briony. 'That's what they call the experts—Skygods. Wouldn't every man like a title like that?'

'It's an illusion,' Ford said dryly. 'Not even the most expert of us could ever be master of the elements.'

'That moment when you are about to fall,' Briony said directly to him, 'are you afraid?'

Ford swirled his drink in his hand, looked into it. 'The time to be afraid is when you've already fallen and there's not a damn thing you can do about it,' he answered wryly.

It was a puzzling note to end on. The conversation

took one of those tangents and Briony was left with the uneasy part-knowledge of something vaguely threatening. What had happened to 'poor old Colin'?

It was another half hour before Briony became aware of Elizabeth Campbell's steady attention. And Margot's. They had obviously swapped stories for Elizabeth was looking daggers at her and Margot wore a certain satisfaction in her protruding eyes. Briony began to get a trapped feeling especially when Stuart deserted her for a few minutes to talk to the trio who had just arrived and were setting up their instruments. She began to drift with the other guests to the buffet when she found Neil beside her. His smile was charming, his eyes insolent.

'Well hello,' he said, 'where did you get to that night? I drove around looking for you.'

And somehow Ford had got the impression that he had found her. 'Did you?'

'Yes. I wanted to find you before Ford did.'

'You mean—he went out——?' she was startled.

Neil gave a sly smile. 'Yes. Elizabeth was furious. She was so mad that I told her I——' he stopped at her expression.

'You told her that you picked me up?' she prompted, but Neil was looking beyond her with a trace of uneasiness.

'Perhaps you'd care to eat now,' Ford said at her shoulder and Briony turned to wither under his iced blue gaze.

Whatever Neil had told Elizabeth had been relayed to Ford in unflattering terms that much was obvious. And now he happened to catch the tail end of a conversation that had an unfortunate intimate sound to it. What a lovely party.

Neil and Ford both disappeared, leaving Briony alone in the laughing, chattering crowd. It was a relief when Stuart turned up again, sliding an arm about her waist in friendly fashion. His arm was about her still next time Ford passed by, his countenance wintry as he registered their closeness. Why—why—she asked herself had she agreed to come tonight?

And she asked herself again a few minutes later when Elizabeth's fluting tones drifted maliciously across the buffet.

'Thank God you've got a decent band tonight, darling,' she laid one hand on Ford's arm. 'That last one you booked—Silversomething—turned out to be rather . . . rough.'

'Oh—oh.' Stuart muttered in Briony's ear as they helped themselves to the drifts of smoked salmon, seafoods and chicken. 'What is your brother's band into? Heavy metal? Punk? And how come our Elizabeth's claws are out of their sheaths?'

'It's a long story,' she told him.

'Heavens,' Elizabeth went on, 'as if it wasn't enough that they provoked those awful louts—one of them actually got into the house.'

One or two people murmured surprise at that. Apparently Elizabeth didn't know that Ford had carried her here. Did she think that she had sneaked into this elegant place and fainted in mid-burgle on the carpet?

'What's this, what's this?' Stuart whispered. 'Got into the homestead did you? You didn't tell me that.'

'How do you know she means me?' Briony demanded, also in a whisper. 'There were four others and the roadies.'

He grinned, 'she's not talking about a man, sweetie.'

Elizabeth's comments ran on, just loud enough to be heard by those opposite. Just modulated enough to maintain the fiction of a private conversation. Briony began to burn. And to hurt. Ford was saying little to discourage the girl's subtle attack. Suddenly she was roaring angry again.

'Hey watch it,' Stuart cautioned. 'You nearly missed your plate with that prawn.'

A little artistic manoeuvring brought Elizabeth quite near and she smiled a bland cocktail party smile as one stranger might to another.

'Have we met?' she asked Briony, and her slight frown was a masterpiece.

'Briony Wilde,' Stuart said helpfully.

'Briony——? From the band? Oh my dear,' the
blonde girl cried, 'I didn't realise when I said—how
embarrassing for you.' To others she might even look
genuine Briony thought, infuriated by the woman's
condescending air.

She shrugged her shoulders. 'Never heard a fing,
ducks,' she said cheerfully. 'Don't yer fret about it.'

There was no answer to that and Elizabeth backed
off, forced into a token smile by the laughter of others
around the table. Even Ford smiled, but that somehow
didn't please Briony as much as it should have. She
took her food and went with Stuart to find a nook in
which to eat it. He acquired two glasses of champagne
which they juggled on a tiny table with their plates.

'How come the Cockney accent?' he asked, and she
told him, keeping it light, funny as if that evening
hadn't marked the turning point in her life. Sighing, she
admitted though that Ford was still suspicious of her.
'I'm sure he thinks I might run off with the silver or
something and I'm afraid things conspire against me.'

'That doesn't exactly surprise me—his suspicions I
mean,' and touched her hand briefly at the look on her
face. 'Not because you look like a crook, Briony pet—
but because of—well—me in a way.'

'You?'

'Yes, Ford's a cynic I guess—partly because of me,
partly because of the business. When he took over from
Dad, you wouldn't believe the graft he found going on
and involving people the old man had trusted for years.
They were robbing the company blind and Ford only
turned the tide by getting tough. It changed him. Of
course, life would have been easier for him if I'd been
prepared to sacrifice my dreams and join him. Ford
studied architecture for a time but abandoned it when
the old man's heart started playing up. But me,' he
smiled ruefully, 'I wanted to play the drums. And I
ignored duty and all the advice and rushed off at
twenty-one to the big time—I thought.'

'Is this the long and——' she stopped.

'Sordid story? This is the one. I joined a group. Ford
didn't like the sound of them from the start but at

twenty-one I was almost unbearably cocky,' he smiled. 'Hard to believe isn't it? Anyway, I auditioned and they snapped me up—for my virtuosity naturally—what else? There was a girl. . . .' He looked out through the glass wall and Briony knew he was looking a lot farther than the ivy-wound lamp outside.

'To cut a long story short—they had plenty of engagements mostly at private functions and it was months before I began to notice something odd about press reports of thefts. "Hey guys," I'd say in my incredible naiveté, "that place we played at last month was burgled," and they'd all look at each other and say "what do you know" and "who cares". I suppose I thought something was wrong when I discovered one of them had a boat he couldn't possibly afford on band earnings and another sported a watch that even Ford might have jibbed at buying. . . .' his eyes went to where his brother stood in conversation. 'Anyway I forgot about my suspicions because Laura—the girl in the band—was suddenly friends, then more than friends. I was crazy about her.' He gave a rueful shake of his head. 'She set me up and I stopped worrying about the odd coincidences. Laura became a habit with me. She even started me on another habit——' he glanced at Briony and nodded at the question in her eyes, 'not the worst I guess, but bad enough. Of course, when the police caught up with them after their latest job—you can guess who had his fingerprints all over the goods.'

Briony's food remained uneaten on her plate. 'Ford had just won a victory, tossing out the company's connivers, and then he had to fight for me. He pinned it on the others eventually—said he couldn't blame me for being taken in by Laura. Big eyes and a little girl's face she had—looked as if butter wouldn't melt in her mouth. . . .'

Briony remembered Ford saying just that to her.

'He kept me out of prison, kept the story out of the press, ran the business and concocted a story to protect our parents from the truth.'

'You mean they didn't know?'

'Still don't. As far as the family is concerned—it

never happened. I was in Melbourne—the folks were abroad. Ford straightened me out again medically and——' he half-smiled, 'morally, I guess. He took up skydiving after all that. I imagine it must have been sublimely relaxing by contrast.'

They both looked at the broad-shouldered figure visible through the knots of guests.

'You went back into a band after all that?'

He nodded. 'Yes. I knew it couldn't happen twice. But Ford has never been certain. Ironic isn't it? It happened to me and I've left it behind. But it left its mark on Ford ... you can see why he might appear unreasonably suspicious of you and your brother's band, Briony.'

And everything she had said would have confirmed his suspicions. She thought of that day when he had chased her on horseback, and the silly, harmless things she'd said to cover her alarm at his appearance. But of course she'd never guessed it could matter at all, let alone that. ...

'End of long and sordid story,' Stuart exclaimed suddenly and pulled her to her feet. 'Let's dance.'

As they moved in time to the easy rhythm of an old standard, Briony looked into Stuart's face.

'Why did you tell me all that?'

His grey eyes rested gently on her. 'Just a feeling I have.'

'Oh, a feeling,' she smiled.

'I heard Ford laughing as he came up the stairs with you—and I saw him put on his armour tonight to hide his feelings. It's a while since I've known him to do either where a woman was concerned.' He grinned down at her. 'He's jealous of me for the first time in my life and I confess I'm enjoying it. Ford has never, never been afraid to leave his lady friends with me.'

'Even if it's true, it doesn't necessarily mean anything,' she protested, trying to quell the hope that flowered at his words.

'Maybe. Maybe not. But the vibes are good. I know. He's different somehow.'

'How do you know I'm not the opportunist he suspects?'

'You forget, sweetie—I've been around the real kind and learned the hard way to tell them apart.'

Briony picked over this new knowledge of Ford. Her eyes found him again and again as she danced with his brother, but he never seemed to look her way. Any hope that he might ask her to dance was dashed when at last she encountered his cool eyes in passing. If it was armour he had put on it was darned near impenetrable she thought.

Margot found her later in the evening at a vulnerable moment. Without Stuart's lazy presence Briony almost backed off from the woman's malice. 'I've been hearing a few things about you tonight, dear. They say men can always recognise your kind. And Gary certainly did. You're nothing but a cheap little groupie.'

Briony turned white.

'You can forget your leisurely job when my aunt hears about you and your provocative act. You'll be out——'

'Margot!' Ford's voice was sharp, his solid warmth suddenly behind her.

'Get your own household in order before you start accusing others. Gary will have me to answer to if he repeats his last mistake. I've already told Doug as much.'

Margot's mouth thinned. She looked expressively from Briony's pale face to Ford. 'I'm beginning to see how it is. How very convenient for you, Ford. Not to mention economical. But not—I fear—up to your usual standard.'

She swept away, leaving her assessment of Briony's place in the scheme of things very clear. It was the final touch to the evening. Briony staggered mentally under the weight of it and tears rushed to her eyes. It didn't help at all when Ford took her arm and looked down at her with that cool reserve that made nonsense of Stuart's hints.

'I apologise for what Margot implied——' he began with a cold formality that pierced like an icicle.

'Why bother? she flung at him. 'It's close enough to the truth after all. Except that you were going to be a little more discreet, weren't you. . . . You were going to "promote" me to some cosy little——' His fingers bit into her arm and she gasped. Ford looked around then drew her into the shadows of the passageway where he held her so tightly that she was barely able to breathe.

'As you don't want apologies,' he bit out, 'perhaps I should re-open the offer. Should you find yourself out of a job you could do worse.'

Desperately Briony hoped she didn't look as pale as she felt. 'Have you had one too many scotches tonight, Ford?' she whispered and wrenched herself from his grasp.

'You're white as a sheet,' Stuart confirmed her fears. 'What the devil did he say to you?'

'Nothing important,' she insisted and somehow she discovered a small, unbruised part of her that talked and smiled and laughed.

It seemed the longest evening in her life—except for that night when she'd looked at Ford in his study and discovered that minutes could slow into hours. At least tonight she thought, there was no carousel playing in ironic gaiety. The guests began to leave. The sound of pampered engines discreetly hummed down the drive followed by others less dulcet. The band stayed for a last drink and Stuart sat at the drums.

'Hey, guys,' he called. 'Do you mind if we jam a little?' They waved their consent and he motioned Briony to a guitar. 'Grab an axe, my pet.'

Oh why not, she thought, looking at the knot of remaining people saying their farewells. Maybe a little music of her own making would alleviate the misery.

'Anything?' she asked Stuart as he tapped the cymbals.

'Anything.'

She began 'Satin Doll' and his eyebrows went up before he closed his eyes and settled into the rhythm. The musicians brought their drinks closer and the bass player quickly got into the act. The other two put aside their drinks and picked up the secondary instruments— an acoustic guitar and flute. They each had their solo, improvising on the classic jazz and it was only as they finished and turned to each other, high on the music, that Briony realised Ford and his overnight guests had come back to listen. Ken and Lila Murray were there too.

'Thanks,' Stuart said to the band and caught Briony about the waist. 'You're fantastic, sweetie. If you ever want a job, just come down to Melbourne.' He kissed her lightly on the lips and let her go and she came back down to earth.

Ken and Lila said goodnight. He leaned close for a moment. 'Judging by your face while you were playing—I would say you already know something of what it's like to be up there.'

She blinked, smiled. 'Then I do understand why you do it.'

His wife said plaintively as they moved away. 'Well then for heavens sake take up the guitar. At least you'd be on solid ground. . . .'

'Will I drive Briony home or will you?' Stuart asked his brother breezily and received a dampening look from his brother.

'I will,' Ford said and went away to return with her coat and bag. He took her arm, his gaze held a moment on the pendant gleaming between her breasts. She just had time to return Stuart's 'Goodnight' when she was steered outside. It was after one and the early morning air was frosty on her skin. She pulled the jacket around her shoulders as she settled in the plush car seat and shivered. It wasn't only the country morning air that chilled. They had been driving for several minutes before he spoke.

'You and Stuart certainly hit it off. I haven't seen him so animated for years,' he said in a dry, formal voice.

Briony turned to look at the hawkish profile. Under that hard exterior she had to remind herself was the man she'd glimpsed now and then. A compassionate man, prepared to shoulder a heavy burden rather than distress his family. Perhaps if things had been different he would have been more carefree, more relaxed like his brother.

'Stuart's a lot of fun,' she said carefully, wondering how to tell him that Stuart was to her the kind of fun that her own brother was. Wondering why, after his renewed insult, it mattered to her.

'Instant relationships seem to be a way of life with you Briony. How long does it take you to make up your mind about a man? No more than one evening apparently.'

'Ford—if you think that Stuart and I——'

Her heart pounded, not bongo drums this time but the thud of a big kettle drum.

'You and Neil—you and Stuart——' he gave a snort of laughter. 'If we hadn't been interrupted that night in my study,' he looked briefly at her, 'it would have been you and I.'

'You're wrong, Ford.'

'Am I? I was about to kiss you that night—a complete stranger. You didn't make any move to stop it. And the next time you certainly didn't.'

'But that was——' she started to say 'different' and the realisation of just how different it was struck her fully, like a door hitting her in the face. Her eyes stared out beyond the beam of the headlights into darkness. Love? No—please. Not that. She strained to see anything past the creamy yellow light. And saw nothing.

'I've never seen Neil except in your study and again tonight. And your brother and I—we get along because we have a few things in common——'

'More than a few I'd say,' he said roughly. He seemed to have lost the cool control that usually governed his speech. 'Whatever it was he was saying to you had you hanging on his every word. I had no idea that Stuart was so fascinating. Or was it just professional talk between two pop aficionados?'

'Some,' she admitted, her eyes fixed on the blackness outside her window. 'He was talking about how you—cared for him when he——'

An exclamation burst from Ford. 'What did he tell you about it?'

'Everything.'

He said nothing and the car passed the road that led to Stocklea Railway Station. She could tell him that she slept there she supposed—follow up the Victorian melodrama of being fed soup and bread in his elegant house by a sojourn on a hard bench for the night. It might at least squash the idea that she spent the night with Elizabeth's cousin. Pride kept her silent. And the knowledge that he probably wouldn't believe her anyway.

'Everything!' He parked the car outside Amy's house and turned off the ignition with a sharp movement. 'What a talent you have for impact, Briony. My shrewd aunt hires you on the strength of a conversation and a cosy letter from some obscure old couple and hands over the keys of her house without a whimper.' In the darkness she could see the glitter of his eyes, the shape of his body turned towards her. 'My cousin has her claws into you and her son propositions you. Elizabeth's cousin fancies you and my brother is enchanted enough to tell you what even the family don't know. Even Ken who rarely tells anyone how he feels, talks to you.'

Briony's carousel had stopped altogether. She'd dropped as far down as she could go and now she wasn't even turning. Her own realisation of her feelings for Ford had served as a brake along with the new, unfair verbal attack of his. Very soon she thought, she would simply get off and put the confusing ride down to harsh experience. . . .

'As for me——' he muttered and left the sentence unfinished as he got out of the car and slammed the door.

Before she knew it she was walking along the drive, his grip on her arm carrying her along with him. The flagstones were a little uneven and Briony gasped as her heels wobbled and one ankle turned. Ford stopped then, took her shoulders and studied her in the cabana light. His eyes dropped to the gold pendant and he picked it up, his long fingers brushing the skin exposed by the dress' low neckline. Marbled pool reflections danced over his face.

'Margot said that this belongs to my aunt.'

Briony stiffened away from his touch and the heavy suspicion in his question.

'She's right. Amy loaned it to me to wear tonight.'

'It's "Amy" now, is it?' he said softly and something snapped in Briony.

She tore away from him, careless for the moment of the pendant he still held. But it swung with her, hitting her in the chest as it slid from his hand.

'Yes, I call your aunt "Amy" at her request. And whatever your cousin might insinuate I haven't stolen any jewellery or anything else from her. I haven't had any kind of relationship with your precious girlfriend's cousin—nor will I have one with your brother.'

He made a move towards her and she backed away, holding out one hand to stay him, clutching her bag and the coat about her shoulders with the other.

'And, Mr High and Mighty Barron, I'd fed up with your supercilious judgments. You invited me to a party tonight, knowing full well that I'd be exposed to the kind of pettiness I experienced . . . you took me to your house and just—left me there among people I didn't know—and some who—h-hated me——' her throat was closing over in spite of her efforts and tears prickled along her eyelids.

Ford stepped forward again and she retreated. 'If it hadn't been for Stuart's unexpected arrival—I would have just been—a fish out of water.'

'Briony, don't——'

'Leave me alone, Ford Barron,' she said fiercely. 'You may be a Skygod up there but you've got a lot to learn on the ground. You've kept me under surveillance and your duty is at an end—here——' she fumbled for the clasp of the pendant, 'take this and then you'll be sure that I——'

His grab for her arm missed as she hunched away from him. Too late Briony saw that her retreat had taken her to the edge of the flagstones. The pendant flipped on its chain as she flailed for balance, reaching for a potted palm and a statue in vain.

Then she toppled into the pool.

CHAPTER EIGHT

THE water closed over her, terrifyingly cold, dragging her down into its dark depths. But she had fallen into the shallow end and her feet touched bottom and her head shot above the surface, long thin strings of hair striping her face.

'Oh—oh——' she spluttered, tears pouring from her face with the pool water. Strong arms slid about her, lifting her over the edge to lean against a warm, wine-coloured shirt on a warm, hard chest.

'Briony,' he almost groaned and picked her up bodily, ignoring the cascades of cold water that poured over his clothes and his expensive, custom-made shoes. He shouldered his way into the cabana bathroom and set her down in the shower recess and turned on the hot water tap. Briony just stood there staring at him, her body quaking with the cold, her dark hair collapsed in sodden rat's tails about her face. Her brain seemed as numb as her body but as the hot water seeped through her dress she collected herself enough to notice that Ford's shirt was soaked and his pants bore large, wet patches.

'Get your clothes off,' he commanded and her hazel eyes widened. 'Where's the key to the caravan?'

'M-m-my bag,' she stammered through frozen lips. 'Did it f-fall in the pool t-too?'

'No,' his lips twitched ever so slightly and Briony could almost imagine he found this amusing. 'I'll bring you some clothes from the van.' He ran those blue eyes over her again and there was a definite laugh in his voice as he mocked her, 'What was that you were saying Briony—about being a fish out of water?'

The glass shower screen slid closed as he went away. She slipped the green dress off and minutes later her shivering decreased under the onslaught of heat and she heard Ford enter the bathroom again. His dark head was blurrily visible through the etched glass and she saw him shrug off the claret shirt and towel himself. Then the glass screen opened.

'I've left a gown for you to wear,' he said and the water streamed down over her body as he made a slow, deliberate study of her. Belatedly Briony turned and her hands went to cover herself but he was gone again.

Towelled dry, but teeth chattering again, she pulled on the dressing-gown he had brought for her. With a towel around her neck to catch the drips from her hair, she went to the van—conscious that she wore not a stitch under the gown. She wrapped the edges closer around her and re-tied the belt, recalling the candid way he had looked at her minutes earlier.

Ford was at the tiny kitchen counter, bare-chested and bare-footed as he poured boiling water into two coffee cups. His expression was unrevealing as he inspected her still-shivering figure. Briony felt a stirring of warmth at the sight of him like this. If he was attractive in his expensive clothes, he was doubly so in this elemental masculine guise.

'Sit down,' he ordered and she subsided on to the padded divan seat. Whipping the towel from her shoulders, he stood over her, rubbing her hair vigorously until her scalp tingled. Pins and slides fell to the floor and he stooped to pick them up. Briony swallowed hard as she looked down at the smoothly muscled shoulders, the powerful line of his back. Her eyes seemed glued to his chest when he stood again and put down the towel.

'Aren't you cold?' she said, and was shocked to hear the husky quality of her voice. What a superb shape he was, she thought and the longing to touch him actually moved her hand towards him as he stood there looking down at her.

Startled, she met his eyes, began to withdraw her hand and disguise the need she had unwittingly revealed. But it was too late. He grasped her wrist, pulled her to her feet and she was inches from him. A wave of desire swept her—its power shocking her all over again. His hands at her waist were warm and strong and possessive. Briony closed her eyes.

'How could I refuse an invitation like that?' he murmured and his hands slipped lower to curve about the swell of her hips, then higher to enclose the ridges of her ribs, then her breasts.

'Ford——' she breathed, hearing the faint trace of sarcasm in his voice. She should protest—tell him that she had only wanted to touch him. It wasn't an invitation . . . not the way he thought . . . the sash of the gown slithered undone and at the touch of his hands on her cold, bare skin, heat coursed through her. An invitation? Hadn't this been what she wanted when she reached out for him?

Ford eased away from her. Slowly he pushed back the edges of the gown and gazed at her, his eyes following the path of his fingers as they lightly traced the lines of breast and midriff, satiny stomach and hips. Her chilled skin burned where he touched and Briony stared at his lowered head. His hair was ruffled, sheening almost black in the van's low light and feeling choked her. Love? she thought again and gasped as he hauled her suddenly tight against him, his hands reaching under the robe to spread over the upper slopes of her buttocks. The belt of his trousers bit into her skin, his rough, warm chest hair rasped against the softness of her breasts. Briony arched towards him, unthinking anymore.

'A rare treat,' he murmured breathily as he nuzzled the length of her neck, 'a girl cold as ice on the outside——' his hands curved lower, bringing her elementally close to him, 'but an inferno inside.'

He kissed her, his mouth already open and seeking symbolic possession. Head fuzzed, heart crazily thumping, Briony returned the kiss with all the fire that had lain dormant—until him. Vaguely she was conscious that her legs were moving—backwards—and then her feet were off the ground altogether and she was on the bed, her gown outflung and skin momentarily cooled by the air. Then Ford covered her with his warmth, length to length and the fire burned more fiercely with his kisses and the potent signals of his body.

Arms around him, she ran her fingers over the ridged

muscles of his back, the steel and satin path of his
spine, nails pressing into him when he put his mouth to
her breast. The sharp, exquisite sensation shot to her
brain and carried with it the unexpected echo of what
he had said. 'Rare treat ... rare treat. ...' No. Her
body denied the careless words. Ford's mouth was
travelling, igniting a trail that wandered over untouched
territory. 'A rare treat. ...' No.

He stood up, his breathing fast and urgent. She heard
the clink of his belt, the staccato sound of a zip.

'No.' She said it aloud at last.

He laughed, low and confidently. 'Ice that is really
fire—no that is really yes ... you mean "yes",
Briony. ...' He bent forward and found her lips,
ruthlessly driving home his point as she instinctively
responded. Another low laugh as he stood and began to
shed the last of his clothes.

Briony sat up, moved to the far wall against which
the bed stood. With shaking hands she folded the gown
across herself, clutched the edges defensively.

'I don't want you to stay, Ford,' she said, the words
forced out. I do. I do—she cried inside, but not to be a
'rare treat'. Not to love him and be another delicacy for
his consumption.

'You—don't—want—me——' he repeated in gravelly
tones. 'Now where did I get the impression that you
did?' Anger crisped each word. In the light shining over
his shoulder he viewed her, curled up like a frightened
kitten against the wall. His hand snaked out and closed
about her arm, jerking her forward so that he could
look into her eyes. 'What changed your mind?' he
demanded and at the mute shake of her head, he
pushed her back against the wall with disgust.

There was silence but for the expressive sounds of his
dressing. At last, bare chested still, he gave her one last
withering look.

'A case of the wrong man perhaps? Maybe I should
have let Stuart bring you home after all.' He grabbed
the edge of the bed curtaining and swished it across,
closing her behind it. Briony sat there watching the
fabric swinging with his force. The van rocked as he

strode from it. Victor scuffled in his cage. Then there was a thump and a sharp, angry curse and the caravan rocked once more. Sitting huddled in her gown, Briony heard Ford go to the cabana and moments later the sound of his re-shod feet crossing the pool flagging.

Tears poured from Briony until her pillow was almost as wet as the green dress hanging in the shower. Somewhere through the window above her bed, there must be stars but she couldn't see one. She crawled under the blankets miserably aware that she was back on the merry-go-round only it wasn't at all merry. And it was going to be a lot harder than she thought to step off. The sky was turning peach by the time she dropped into sleep. And in her head the mocking strains of the carousel's song played over and over ... 'It's the loveliest night of the year. . . .'

When Victor woke her, she sat up hopefully. A bad dream she insisted. Then she looked down at the dressing-gown she wore and through the bed curtains to the two eloquent coffee mugs on the kitchen table. One was half full, the other hardly touched, its surface wrinkled.

The Sunday tranquillity closed about number eighteen Sandalwood Street but Briony remained immune to the deep peace. Ford weighed heavy on her mind. But when she'd run through last night and her own emotions a dozen times or more, she spared a thought for her immediate future. When she picked up Amy from the station, she would have to tell her about the band and the Gala night before Margot did. What the old lady's reaction would be she didn't like to think, but in a way it would be a relief to level with her. Amy was one person who liked directness and she would have every right to resent the lies of ommission of an employee.

Briony went out and dug up the strip of garden that bordered the van either side of the steps. Eventually she threw down the fork, feeling close to howling and walked briskly to visit George in his neat house a few streets away. Not as prosperous as Amy's, it was cosy and appealing, nestled in the lush garden that he had created.

He was out among his plants, inspecting them through his bifocals, pipe in full furnace. Briony walked around with him half-listening to his easy conversation and gardening hints.

'I've got some phlox and petunia seeds, George. Is it too early to plant them do you think?'

He chewed on his pipe, then shook his head. 'Should be all right if you watch out for a late frost. But if you're wanting something to do to keep your mind off things, you can tidy up the bush house plants. Lot of dead leaf on the ferns in Amy's baskets.'

'Yes—I'll do that.'

'Didn't go so well, eh? The party?'

'Oh. The party.' She poked at the stone edge of a garden bed with one toe. 'Yes and no. I met Stuart.'

'Ah he's back is he?' George smiled. 'Charming young scamp.' He looked at her, waiting as if he knew she had something to say.

'I played with that band you know, George. Silverhero. The one that caused such a ruckus at Ford's Gala.'

The old man's eyebrows went up. He even took his pipe from his mouth. 'Well, well. I thought I saw glitter on your eyes that night. So that's why you're so expert on that guitar, eh?' He eyed her glum expression. 'Worried about Amy knowing?'

She nodded.

'You could have told her, love. She prefers Gilbert and Sullivan but she wouldn't fire you for playing rock and roll.'

But the old-fashioned look he gave her made it clear that he had grasped the intricacy of the situation. Ford had known all about it and not said a thing. It did look odd.

'Don't let him hurt you, Briony,' he murmured and his eyes squinted behind the smoke as he drew again on his pipe.

Too late, she thought—too late. It must have shown in her eyes for George peered over his bifocals at her.

'Now that's too bad,' he said. 'That's no good at all.'

The fern baskets were duly dead-leafed and the seeds

planted in the garden by the van. Briony tamped down the soil and sprayed the smooth beds wondering if she would be here to see the flowers bloom. Victor was singing in his cage when she went to pick up Amy.

All the way from the station Briony looked for a chance to tell Amy. But the old lady was full of her weekend away and enthused about her next visit to her friend, planned to coincide with the Bowral Tulip Festival in October, so that she had no opportunity. Only as they turned into Sandalwood Street did she ask: 'And how did you enjoy Ford's party my dear?'

It was the perfect cue to confess but as Briony swung the car into Amy's drive, her heart sank. Margot Drewett was just stepping from her Mercedes and her sons were already at the gate.

'Amy,' she said in a rush, 'I didn't tell you everything about myself when I came here.'

'Well I knew that, Briony,' came the calm reply. 'Could you bring in my parcels for me my dear?' she added with a sigh as she turned to greet Margot. The woman ignored Briony but for a narrow, spiteful glance and they all went inside.

Any hope of a quiet sorting out of the matter was firmly put aside by Margot who broached it as soon as they were indoors. She took considerable satisfaction from her discomfort Briony thought. So did the abominable sons.

'I think it only right to put you in possession of the facts, Aunt Amy. This girl,' she said the word bitingly, 'has been running around with a rock-and-roll band wearing nothing more than a few sequins and boots. Anything Gary said to her, she asked for.'

'Rock and roll?' Amy exclaimed mildly, 'Well for heaven's sake. And you play such wonderful classical pieces my dear. But surely,' she paused eyes bright with curiosity and well aware how her casual reaction was irritating Margot, '—more than just a *few* sequins?'

'And that means, Aunt, in case you haven't thought of it, that Ford knew about her all along. She played at the Gala.'

Shrewd grey eyes speared Briony, but Amy was saving her questions until later. 'Yes, it does, doesn't it?'

Margot tried again. 'I don't like to be the one to point out to you darling, that it isn't a very—respectable situation. If he wants to have his mist——'

'That'll do Margot.' The old lady signed Briony to go and she began to do so gratefully, conscious of Margot's rising resentment at Amy's attitude. Briony felt a wave of guilt. She hardly deserved Amy's support on that last accusation. After all she could quite easily have become Ford's mistress last night ... if he had remained silent. Her face was heated as she passed Margot and the woman's baleful eyes followed her.

'And I hope you brought back that emerald pendant,' she said petulantly.

Briony stopped in her tracks. The pendant! She'd forgotten all about it. Her mind raced to remember where she'd put it but she could only conjure up images of Ford carrying her to the shower, telling her to remove her clothes. ... Stricken, she turned to Amy and Margot moved in quickly on her uncertainty.

'You haven't lost it?'

'No. Of—of course not.'

'Where is it then?' Margot demanded.

'I—er—oh, Amy, I can't think where I put it. I had it on when we came home. Then—I might have taken it off before I fell in the pool——'

There was dead silence. 'Fell in the pool, my dear?' Amy asked.

She was beetroot red now. 'Oh yes—I slipped.'

'That must have been chilly.' The old lady's eyes were full of speculation. 'I hope Stanford got you into a hot shower quick and lively?'

Margot made a sound of disgust.

'Oh yes—that is, I did. I must have taken the pendant off when——'

'It will turn up my dear. It can't have gone far.'

Amy, Briony couldn't help thinking, was probably more interested to know just how far she—and Ford—had gone rather than the pendant. At the moment anyway.

The pendant didn't turn up. Briony searched the pockets of her sodden coat, searched her bag and the ground around the caravan. The Drewett boys hung about enjoying her distraction.

'She must have an accomplice to get rid of the goods so fast,' Gary remarked to his brother. 'What an act, pretending to have lost it.'

'Unless she's got it in her van.'

She gritted her teeth and said nothing. It was her fault. Her preoccupation with Ford had wiped any clue as to the jewellery's whereabouts from her memory.

Later, in a sombre mood, she returned the canary to his leafy paradise in Amy's sun room and stopped for tea over which she was reprimanded for not admitting she'd met Ford previously.

'And I'll be having a word with Stanford about that too,' she declared then went on to quizz her about last night and her years with the band. Unable to elaborate on the first, Briony talked about Silverhero and Jeff's previous groups—about her job at Rocco's and her guitar lessons. And the Gala.

'Your nephew blamed me for the trouble with those boys at the time, but he was——'

'Yes? He was?'

'Well I fainted you see—and he was helpful. Kind.' Briony said inadequately.

Amy pursed her lips. 'Kind. Well that's nice to hear that he was—er—kind. I hope——' she hesitated. 'No, it doesn't matter.'

Maybe that was a question she would reserve for Ford, Briony thought. What would he tell her, she wondered as she went back to her van.

Absently she watered the soil where she'd planted her seeds that morning, thinking of Ford and a mislaid emerald. The outline of a footprint didn't immediately register with her. She stared at it, close by the van steps—a ribbed, medium-size foot, toe out coming away from the van as if someone had jumped in a shortcut from the top step. Not hers. And it hadn't been there when she'd smoothed the earth over her seeds.

The caravan seemed untouched. The contents as she'd left them. Her clothes were tidily away and the loose change lying beside the bed with a few hairslides and elastics for her hair hadn't been touched. All the same a sick, violated feeling persisted in her stomach as if she knew someone had been in here, touching her things—opening and shutting cupboard doors.

'Watch out for a spider in your bed' Stuart had warned and she recalled the two boys hanging around, idle and full of malice. She flung back the sheets and blankets and found nothing. Shook out her gum boots, checked the wardrobe. Not a thing. Briony took a deep breath. There was no point in mentioning it to Amy. She had no proof that the boys had been in after all, save the footprint. It would only distress the old lady.

That night Briony jumped at the small creakings and sighings outside. The footprint boldly set in her garden so close to her door, reminded her of her vulnerability. So she lay awake long after midnight, nervous of every night bird's screech and reliving the confusing scene with Ford. Her pillow was damp under her cheek when she slept and she dreamed of falling, falling and looking up in vain for the blossom of a parachute above her.

Restless night followed restless night. There was no sign of Ford. No sign either of the pendant. Amy didn't seem too bothered about it. 'It must be around somewhere,' she said and dismissed Margot's insinuations with her usual disregard for her niece's opinion. 'How my sister and her man—God rest their souls— ever produced Margot I'll never know,' she said and that was that. She was far more concerned with Ford's increased activities as a member of Apollo.

'He's replacing a team member who broke a leg,' she told Briony. 'Quite badly I believe—in three places.'

So that was what happened to Colin. 'Then he was lucky,' Briony said, imagining Ford swathed in bandages. 'It's a dangerous sport.'

'Oh he didn't break it parachuting dear. No, apparently he fell off a ladder while he was painting his kitchen ceiling.'

Briony laughed. There was something farcical about an intrepid skydiver sustaining multiple fractures in his kitchen. But she sobered quickly. The odds would be heavily against that normally. Ford's little talked-about sport hadn't seemed real until she had spoken to Ken Murray. With her abrupt recognition of her feelings for Ford, had come a vivid, tearing comprehension of the danger he invited each time he launched himself into the air. What must it be like to fall into nothingness— what did it take to trust yourself to no more than a few slender cords and a square of nylon? How could she have ever joked about his parachute . . . was he even now falling through space, risking his neck——?

'—filming some of the practice sessions I'm told,' Amy was saying. 'But Saturday's jump is the final and the one the cameras want an audience for. I think I'll go.'

Briony drove the old lady to Ford's house on the day and even as late as that, hadn't made up her mind to go with her to the drop zone. After all Stuart was going and her own presence wasn't required as Amy's driver. If she went, Ford would know it was from choice and after their last meeting that could be embarrassing.

They were early and Ford was ready to leave as they drove up his sweeping drive. The Land Rover stood by the house and he bundled a large zippered bag into it and turned at the sound of Amy's car. His greeting was abrupt, reluctant. Dressed in a chest-hugging skivvy and slim pants in black he looked different again. Today there was a new tension about him. Briony studied him. It was the tight-coiled awareness of what he would do, she guessed. As if he was already up there, sharpening himself mentally for the confrontation with—with what? What did he think about before he played with life and death? Whatever it was, her instincts told her that their presence was intrusive. His preparations needed only himself. Demanded it.

It was with embarrassment then that she stepped out of the car when Stuart loped from the house and opened her door. For Amy, shrewd in so many ways, had not read Ford's signals and was already chattering to him—warning him good luck and wishing him and referring him to a half dozen other sports less dangerous. 'Golf,' she was telling him, 'now you'd be a top player Stanford if you played regularly. And you'd look more relaxed going to golf than you do now. . . .'

'For heavens sake,' Briony muttered to Stuart, 'get your aunt inside for coffee or something.' Stuart glanced at his brother's tight face.

'I see what you mean.'

Cheerfully he diverted Amy and Briony stood awkwardly by the car as they went inside. Ford slammed the door of the Land Rover and looked over at her. She was wearing a scarlet jump-suit—an unconsciously ironic choice—over a thin cream sweater. Her hair had tucked away under a matching red cap and Briony put up a hand to a dark escaping strand that tickled her cheek.

'Are you coming? To watch?' he asked unsmilingly.

'No,' she shook her head, making up her mind right then and there that she would. Had to.

'Good,' he grunted, 'in that outfit you'd be a beacon at five thousand feet.' On that sarcastic note he swung into the driver's seat and drove off, his face settling into lines of fierce concentration.

The drop area was ringed about by spectators and enthusiasts. A television vehicle and helicopter were parked away from the cars.

'The chopper will take up a camera to film the last few thousand feet of the fall,' Stuart told her. 'Ford and the others aren't too happy about that.'

Briony didn't ask why. She didn't have to. A parachutist tangling with chopper blades made a clear enough picture. Luckily Amy didn't hear. She was talking to an old crony and Elizabeth Campbell who sent Briony a discouraging look and Stuart one only slightly warmer.

'Can't tear yourself away from home, Stu?' she said with false sweetness, detaching herself from Amy and friend.

'I had to stay to see Ford take the plunge, Liz,' he said and his reciprocal abbreviation of her name apparently displeased her. Her pale eyes travelled to Briony.

'Well keep a close watch—if you look in the wrong direction you could miss it altogether.'

Stuart grinned. 'I think I can follow Ford's drift.'

'As I said—watch carefully,' she repeated and strolled away, elegant in her slim pants and classic blazer to join a group which included Lila Murray.

The cameras in the drop plane and in another aircraft following were probably already rolling, Stuart told Briony as two specks approached the drop area. Her stomach turned over. There was a ripple of noise among the spectators, led by those with binoculars.

'They're out,' someone yelled and Briony saw a few faint dots beneath the larger plane, falling rapidly then bunching, but any order quite undetectable here almost ten thousand feet below. They perfect their sport, she thought angrily—risk their lives and no one can appreciate their precision; what a stupid sport! But their separation was clearer. Six dots dived apart, their levels altering and Stuart prised open her fist to put binoculars in her hand. 'Ford's chute is indigo and yellow,' he said softly as the para-wing canopies bloomed against a china sky. Four canopies, five.

'I can't see one that colour,' she jerked out at last, the glasses following the one diver still dropping through the air. It was Ford. It had to be. Shaking she thrust the field glasses at Stuart and stared helplessly at the plummeting figure. The crowd had moved as one towards the marked landing area and the helicopter clattered overhead. Why were they all talking so—so normally, she thought? Couldn't they see a man falling to his. . . . Briony couldn't take it any longer. She whirled around, eyes closed and didn't notice that she was left alone on the grass-covered ground, the light breeze plucking at her red jumpsuit.

Stuart came back for her. 'Its all right—its okay— look.' He turned her around and she saw the yellow and indigo stripes of a chute carrying a figure towards the strip. 'Steady Briony—you're shaking like a leaf.'

'I just thought—I was sarcastic to him once about checking his parachute . . .' she attempted to smile but her eyes didn't leave the fast drifting figure of Ford. He was approaching the field from a wide angle, almost overhead, and though he had been last to inflate, was second to land. The first man came down, rolled once and hurried aside, gathering in his lines and Lila Murray dashed past waving to her husband.

When Ford landed, Briony almost felt the thump. She clutched Stuart and his arm went about her in support.

'He's okay,' he said again. 'Hasn't landed well though—that's not like him.'

The yellow and indigo stripes bubbled over an inert body and several men moved in to carry Ford away from the target as another parachutist approached.

'Stuart,' Amy said beside them in blissful ignorance, 'what colour is Ford's parachute?'

She got no answer until they saw Ford coming from the field, supported by Ken Murray and another man.

'Thank God,' Amy said fervently, 'I wish he'd take up golf.'

Briony said nothing but she held on to Stuart's waist as if she might fall otherwise. So this was what it was like—her eyes sought out Lila Murray's ecstatic face. Agony and reprieve. People crowded forward as the other members of Apollo landed. Ford's eyes settled on Briony and Stuart, their arms about each other's waists. He was limping and cursing softly, his face pale and grim.

'How the hell did you manage that, Ford?' Ken asked. 'You never muff landings.'

Dimly Briony heard the whirring of a camera, felt the rush of air as the helicopter flew over. Ford glanced up and met her eyes for a moment.

'I lost concentration,' he snapped. Amy planted a kiss on his cheek and he nodded at Stuart and Briony then limped into the sympathetic arms of Elizabeth Campbell.

'Darling—I never get used to your courage,' she kissed him lingeringly on the mouth, positioned perfectly for the camera, and it seemed awfully one-sided, until Ford managed to stand on his injured foot to put both arms about her and return the kiss with enthusiasm.

'But your poor leg,' Elizabeth pouted when at last Ford raised his head. 'You won't be able to dance with me tonight.'

Stuart looked down at Briony and gave her a brotherly squeeze. She hardly felt it. The flame blue of his brother's eyes met hers fleetingly again then he smiled at Elizabeth. 'We'll think of something,' he said.

Before they left, Lila Murray made her way to Briony. She touched her hand briefly and smiled. 'The first time's the worst. It's not only the men who discover the self they didn't know.' She was gone before Briony could protest—could pretend that her stricken face had been for something else—that this 'first' was also a 'last'. That her discovery was only confirmation and a hopeless one at that.

A sprained ankle, Briony found out later, was Ford's only injury. He had gone back to work and his city apartment and she was glad. Perhaps by the time she saw him again she would have control of her emotions. Stuart had gone too. Back to the band and the lure of success. The ridiculous fantasies roused by his hints at the party rapidly faded. So did her hopes of finding Amy's emerald.

Weekends passed and Ford stayed away. Her prayer plant threw up a beautiful leaf of newborn green. The Japanese maple showed the merest signs of budding. The frog croaked every night near the pool.

Then Amy announced that they would go up to Sydney for the day.

'I need to see my solicitor about some property,' she said. 'And do a bit of shopping.'

'Do you need a gardener with you to do that, Amy?' Briony enquired with a smile.

'Of course. I may want you to carry a few parcels for me.'

'I'll bet Harry didn't go to town with you.'

'Harry had his limitations. He was not at home in boutiques.'

'Single tickets?' Briony questioned when they reached the railway ticket box on Friday morning.

'That's right my dear. We're coming back by car tonight. Stanford will drive us home.'

Tension gripped her throat and she said nothing as they boarded. She gazed out the train window at pastureland and tiny farmhouses but saw a bronzed face with piercing blue eyes. It was unlikely they would have anything to say to each other with Amy there. Just as well.

With a start she noticed that Amy was talking. '. . . and he wants me to consider the investment. He's a canny boy so I imagine it will be gilt-edged.'

Briony assumed this must be the solicitor and Amy confirmed it. 'I've known Gerry and Louise for years and I'm godmother to their second girl. Dear old Milly is her godfather,' Amy sighed.

On their arrival in Sydney, Amy took a cab to her solicitor's office after they had arranged to meet at a restaurant for lunch. Briony browsed in the shops, bought a paperback and strolled through Hyde Park. Watching the fountains, she thought how ironic it was that she had never seen the city's beauty while she lived in it. Even the noise seemed less objectionable now that there was Stocklea to return to. At eleven-thirty she phoned Jeff and laughed at the sleepy sound of his voice.

'Just out of bed?' she chided.

'Worked two shows last night,' he mumbled and yawned. 'The last one didn't finish until one.'

'And then you had a bit of a jam session, a few drinks . . .' she laughed.

'Yeah, yeah—so you know all about us muso's. How's business with Mrs Whatsername? Everything in the garden lovely?'

'Sure. I'm in town with Mrs Gordon today, shopping.' Her offhand reply seemed to snap Jeff from his sleepiness.

'Thing not so good, Bry?'

'Fine. Why would you think that?'

'Brotherly intuition. That cautious note in your voice wouldn't be anything to do with a man would it?'

She laughed. 'Why do men always think its one of them that's the cause when a woman is a bit low?'

'Not like you to be low, Bry. Tell you what—we leave on our tour soon. I'll send you the key in case you come haring back to Sydney.'

'No need, Jeff. Oh, by the way—how did you know about trimming carnations?'

'Just another gem I've collected in my chequered career, m'dear. Wait until I tell you my way with chrysanthemums.'

Briony was early at the restaurant and ordered coffee while she waited for Amy who arrived late, pink cheeked and sparkling.

'You'll never guess—Gerry and Louise have a spare ticket to the *Mikado* tonight and they've asked me to go. You won't mind my dear, will you? I adore Gilbert and Sullivan and especially the *Mikado*. It's not done much these days so I must take advantage of it. Afterwards I'll stay the night with them and Maree, my goddaughter, is going to drive me home tomorrow.' She beamed and began to hum 'Three Little Maids' much to the surprise of the waiter.

'That's marvellous, Amy,' Briony said and it was a moment before it hit her. She would have to go home tonight to Stocklea alone. Not alone. With Ford. A feeling of panic set in. A two-hour drive without Amy as a buffer was not something she'd bargained on.

'Anything wrong, Briony?' Amy asked.

'No. Of course not. But perhaps I could take the train back as you won't be going.'

'Heavens no. Stanford's going to Abingdon for the weekend anyway. I've already phoned him and he will be expecting you at his office.' Her clever grey eyes swept over Briony in sudden doubt. 'You're looking very pretty today my dear,' she said somewhat irrelevantly. 'That cream outfit suits you very well.' Amy appeared to have second thoughts about sending her home with her nephew, but the lure of Gilbert and Sullivan was strong and she said nothing more.

After lunch they embarked on a spending spree that had Briony's head whirling. Amy dealt out credit cards at any number of stores and by the time they parted company after five o'clock at Gerard Walter's office, they were each carrying a pile of boxes and parcels.

'Tell Stanford to drive carefully. I don't wish to lose either of you,' Amy said as she left the cab with half the parcels. She leaned in to give the driver the address of the Barron Building. 'Don't fall in the pool again, will you, Briony?' There was a wealth of warning in the words.

Ford's office was fronted by a reception area—a lush pasture of long-piled carpet dotted with superb, austere furniture. Behind the gleaming chrome and perspex desk was a smoothly groomed woman of about Ford's age—mid-thirties at any rate. She seemed flustered as she put her hand over the phone's mouthpiece.

'Miss Wilde? Mr Barron will be tied up for a while. Won't you sit down?'

Amy's parcels went every which way as Briony sat on a sleek visitors' divan. The woman at the desk spoke in a low voice on the phone.

'Yes darling, I'll be there just the moment I can get away. Mr Barron wants a letter to go tonight and I can't just walk ... well of course I want to be there when he—explain to him for me—that I ... no I can't make the early bus. It leaves in ten minutes and I have to type ... as fast as I can get there, then. Bye.'

With a glance at her watch, the woman turned a page in her shorthand notebook and set paper in the typewriter. She caught Briony's eye and grimaced. 'Sorry about all that. Most unprofessional. Its just that the hospital is letting my son come home tonight instead of tomorrow. He had both legs broken in an accident and ...' she smiled in embarrassment and began to type, only to snatch the paper from the rollers with a muffled exclamation. She smoothed back her hair in a nervy gesture and Briony felt a stab of sympathy.

'How old is he?'

'Jamie's six,' she smiled guiltily, her mother's mind already flying ahead to her son's homecoming, while she tried to play her secretary's role. Briony stacked up Amy's new spring wardrobe on the divan and waited a moment to check that the parcel pyramid did not move.

'Let me do it,' she went over to the desk and ran her eye over the shorthand notes. 'Is that word there "expedite"?'

The woman nodded. 'Yes, but——'

'And how do you style Mr Barron in his letters—"Managing Director"?'

'Yes, but——'

'Really its okay. I have to sit and wait anyway. And you need to go to your son.'

'Thanks a million. And my name's Marion by the way ... and there are some stamps in the drawer ...' she was gone in a whiff of Tweed.

Briony took her seat, savouring the peculiar circumstances of acting as Ford's secretary. At least it took her mind off the long drive home as she typed the letter.

The door marked BARRON was closed upon the murmur of men's voices. She was on the last few lines of the letter when the door opened and Ford came out with another man. He didn't see her at first, no doubt assured by the sound of the typewriter that Marion was at her desk. But his gaze fell upon the parcels on the divan then moved sharply to her and his expression was almost comical. The nearest she'd seen to his open-mouthed surprise was when he'd cracked Amy's wall. But he recovered and strolled to the glass doors with his visitor and saw him out. He wasn't limping, she noticed.

He turned back to her, remaining by the door and viewing her across the beige expanse of carpet.

'Where's Marion?' he asked as she rolled the completed letter from the IBM.

'Taken the early bus to be home in time for her son. Jamie's coming out of hospital this afternoon. I've done the letter you wanted.'

Ford blinked. 'How long were you waiting out here?'

'About five minutes.'

'And she told you all that?'

Briony shrugged. 'Another instant relationship, I guess,' she said dryly. At least this one he couldn't misconstrue.

Without moving, he studied her. He had begun to say something when his phone rang and he strode into his office again.

Briony typed an envelope, clipped it to the letter and went to the office door when she heard Ford hang up. Knocking, she walked in to put the letter on the massive leather-topped desk. Ford leaned back in his swivel chair and for once seemed unsure of himself. She couldn't resist it.

'Will that be all, Mr Barron?' she gave him her wide-eyed attentive secretary look, deliberately over-playing the part. He pulled the letter towards him, uncapped a pen and signed it after a brief perusal.

'No that's not all, Miss Wilde. Will you have dinner with me?'

It was part of the game she supposed, and she had started it. 'Oh no, sir. I could never date the boss.'

The flame blue eyes warmed, laugh lines fanned at their corners. 'In that case you're fired. And now that we're strangers again—how about dinner? I'd—like to get to know you.'

A new start? Was that what he was saying? Briony felt warmth rush to her face and her flippancy vanished.

'I—I'd like that.'

'Half an hour—do you mind waiting?'

She shook her head. Mind? Didn't the sound of her heart's drumbeat tell him that she would wait a great deal longer than that?

CHAPTER NINE

A SWEET, anticipatory forty minutes later, she was in Ford's car and among the traffic. Briony looked about and wondered how she had ever hated the clogged streets—there was something beautiful in the crooked lines of traffic lit here and there by a premature headlight in the dusk, and the towering buildings— dusty pseudo-gothic and stainless steel. A slanted glance at the man next to her gave her the source of this new, rosy picture of Sydney's commercial heart. She wondered if she had overdone the perfume, hoped that her cheeks—pink with excitement—and her eyes—too bright when she had checked her reflection in a Powder-Room mirror—were not giving her away.

When they stopped for a moment she caught a glimpse of herself, a cameo in the frame of Ford's car window reflected in a storefront, and even from here she could see the naive wideness of her eyes. Careful— she warned and smoothed back her hair that fell loose to her shoulders and seemed to be her only feature to remain unaffected by this turn of events.

'Don't forget to post that letter,' she reminded him prosaically. He pulled in at the next post box, among outraged beepings, and dropped the envelope in. Starting the car again, he mocked: 'Quite the perfect secretary even after you've been fired. Amy told me you'd had an office job. I wasn't sure if it was true.'

Some of the rose colour went from the evening at his assumption she might have lied but she answered lightly: 'Well it is. I did a year of night school and worked five years in offices. Playing in the band was a nights and weekends business.'

'So you haven't been roughing life on the road since you were fourteen,' he murmured and seemed rather amused.

'I only said that because—well, you seemed to expect it. And I never thought I'd see you again——'

He nodded thoughtfully and wove his way through the traffic heading across the Harbour Bridge.

'And I believe you're not an orphan after all?'

Briony grimaced. 'No. But our parents—well, they're not really involved with us.' And she mentioned the annual letters, the one visit in five years, the preoccupation of them with their mutual misery together, then later with their new, separate lives. 'Jeff and I were sharing a flat as soon as I left school. Then he went off on his own and I went to board with the McPhersons which was more like home than home had been . . . then I ended up in my own flat when they sold their house.'

'And then—Stocklea.'

'Yes,' she smiled and her tone said it all. 'Then Stocklea.'

After a few minutes Ford said, 'I have to apologise for what I said and did that first day I saw you at Amy's place. My only excuse is that I felt I had to make certain that her interests were protected.'

'Oh—er——' she stammered.

'And I may have over-compensated for my conflict of interest.'

'Conflict?'

They were stationary at traffic lights and Ford turned to her. 'I felt it was my duty to move you on just in case you were up to no good. But my natural inclination was to keep you there.'

'Oh,' she gulped.

'So—feeling I was compromising my ideals I guess I was rather harsh on you.'

She remembered just how harsh he had been. How she had lashed out at him in fury and pain that he could think so little of her.

'I nearly had my revenge,' she reminded him and he laughed.

'Later I wished you had hit me,' he admitted. 'It might have made me feel less of a brute.'

'Well, just let me know if you still feel bad. I can

always arrange a right to the jaw,' she grinned, trying to hide the racing exhilaration beneath her humour.

He chuckled. 'I guess I owe you the opportunity of that. But please—not in the restaurant.'

The restaurant was certainly not the kind of place for a scene. Any such ideas of violence would be quietly, determinedly depressed beneath the iron gentility of the place. Only the music ousted the impression of an exclusive club room. They went first to the bar, opted for two deep, seductive chairs and ordered drinks in response to a hushed enquiry from the waiter.

Ford lifted his glass to her and though he smiled, there was tension in him, holding his shoulders taut. His hands were tight, one bunched along the arm of his chair, the other gripping his glass with unconscious grimness. Over her drink she viewed the lines around his eyes and realised why Amy worried about him. He looked as if he'd worked solid since his last stay at Abingdon and that jump that had almost gone wrong.

'You look tired.' She could have bitten her tongue. She hoped the words wouldn't sound as wifely to him as they did to her.

'Its been a tough few weeks. Business lately makes skydiving seem like a pleasant country stroll.'

She prompted him to talk and he did, his tension diminishing as he touched with dry humour on the difficulties of running a large family business.

'Need I say more than that Margot is on the Board?' he said and she laughed.

'For the first time this week I feel relaxed,' Ford said.

'It's Friday,' she smiled. 'And you're going home for the weekend.'

His eyes almost closed. 'No I don't think that's the reason. Shall we eat?'

As they went to the table his arm was lightly about her waist. 'Careful' a weak little voice said in Briony's head.

Each table was separated from its neighbours by discreet placement of four-winged screens so that they were private on at least two sides. A small band played and Briony moved her head to see the musicians but could only make out a pianist and bass guitarist immaculately attired in matching grey suits and burgundy frilled shirts. The drummer and second guitarist she could not see because of the intervening screens. The music was a laid-back jazz sound with some subtle improvisations from the piano and the unseen guitarist. Good, she thought. Very good. Her eyes came back to find Ford watching her.

'Friends of yours?'

'No.'

'You played superbly with Stuart and the trio at my place,' he commented. 'I meant to tell you how much I enjoyed your jam session.'

Briony gave a laugh. 'So jazz is more your style than rock. You didn't look as if you were enjoying it though.'

That was an understatement. He'd looked black as thunder.

He didn't answer that. After a moment or two he said: 'I should never have taken you to that party. It was the wrong time and the wrong people were present. But I wanted you there—a typically selfish move on my part.'

'Typically?' she repeated. 'Selfishness doesn't seem to be your major fault. In fact, according to Stuart. . . .'

'I'm no hero, in spite of what Stuart might have told you. Don't get any ideas of me as a selfless saint,' he advised her roughly.

'I won't.' Her prompt, dry answer lifted his frown. 'Do you worry about him still, Ford? Stuart I mean?'

He thrust his lower lip forward and studied his drink. 'Yes, I suppose I always fear he might slip back——'

'No.' Briony shook her head. 'Not now. Stuart's not the type to make the same mistake twice.'

'Not like me, you mean?' he said wryly, but she could see him clutching at her words. How terribly lonely for him not being able to talk to anyone about it—not to be offered the bulwark of another opinion.

'I hope you're right. Staying in the pop business lays him open to the same risks.'

'Jumping from a plane is a risk,' she pointed out.

'But you keep doing it. And even then you only got a sprained ankle. "Poor old Collin" sustained multiple fractures painting his kitchen.' She shrugged. 'That's life.'

He looked gravely at her for a moment, then smiled. She fancied his burden might have shifted a fraction.

'I just hope I don't lose my concentration next time I jump,' he murmured, going off at a tangent, 'or I'll get worse than a sprain.'

'Why did you?'

His eyes were mocking. 'A scarlet beacon put me off.'

Briony's eyes opened wide. 'A beacon at five thousand feet,' he'd said. Had she distracted him? Hardly likely. She bit her lip ostentatiously.

'I'd never forgive myself if you injured yourself because of what I wore,' she paraphrased his own words neatly and he laughed.

'You suffered no ill effects from your last fall I hope?' he said after a while. 'Into the pool.'

That depended on what he meant by 'ill effects' she supposed. She sometimes regretted that she'd sent him away . . . Briony wished she hadn't thought of that. The darned bongo drums had started up again.

'No. The green dress will never be the same again though. I suppose I should thank you for rescuing me—again.'

His tone was dry. 'My "rescues" seem to go awry somehow.'

Briony flushed.

'Or is it my timing that's all wrong lately,' he murmured, his gaze wandering over her face.

'It can't be,' she said too brightly, 'Not with all that precision relative work you've been doing.'

'Yes, up in the blue I can usually make contact.'

Briony picked up her wineglass and looked into it with great concentration. 'Maybe—you're misjudging the level of your—um——'

'Target?' he grinned. 'Yes, I'm beginning to think that's my problem.'

The meal came as a welcome relief from all this double talk and the too quick effect of an excellent wine. They ate in silence, but an easy one, as the music of the four-piece combo flowed around them.

'How was your meal?' he asked as they finished.

'Wonderful. But I've tasted better.'

A dark eyebrow rose at this breach of good manners. 'Oh?'

'Mmmm. The best meal I've ever had was soup and bread and hamburgers served by a forbidding gentleman.'

'Forbidding?' he looked mildly annoyed. 'Surely not?'

'Definitely forbidding and . . . nice, too.'

'Nice,' he grunted and turned his mouth down at the corners.

'What's wrong with forbidding and nice?' she asked innocently. 'Anyway, he was rather good-looking as well.'

Ford leaned his chin on his hand, his eyes bright with amusement.

'Well now—that's better,' he said. 'Did he have anything else to recommend him.'

'Well yes,' Briony admitted, 'He had a sort of—aura about him . . .'

'Ah.'

'. . . I think it was his after shave.'

The dessert arrived and Briony tackled the hot-house strawberries and cream with unabashed enthusiasm and a mental warning to guard her tongue. The wine was making her forget that Ford could just be amusing himself.

'You do enjoy your food don't you? I can't remember when I last saw a woman devour a sweet with so much relish. Most of the ones I know are always dieting.'

'But then I'm not like the women you know am I? Mr Ford Barron is not usually seen with unsophisticated girls like me, I imagine.'

'Is that what you are?'

'An unsophisticated guitar player turned odd-job girl—that's me,' she said blithely, suddenly compelled to point out the difference between them. More for her own benefit than anything else.

Ford signalled to a waiter and ordered coffee and liqueurs.

'You seem to be very certain of my tastes in women. They're not at all as predictable as you might think. For instance I almost made quite a fool of myself over the merest child not long ago. At least I thought she was the merest child.'

'Oh yes?' she murmured and felt her pulses quicken.

'She had a beautiful figure—long legs. A fantasy girl. Hair that was crinkled mahogany satin and sparkling hazel eyes. Dressed in a ridiculous outfit with boots. When I saw her,' he smiled ruefully, 'I kept going back to look even though I knew I was being a fool . . . a mature man with a crush on a cute little groupie maybe half my age.'

Briony felt dizzy. Had the contempt on his face that night been for himself?

'Fortunately she turned out to be older than I thought which made me feel better.'

'And what happened?'

'Oh, I was cured the moment she spoke to me,' he said gravely. 'She had the most awful Cockney accent.'

'Just as well. She sounds entirely unsuitable for a man in your position.'

'You think so?' Before she could answer, he rose and held out a hand to her. 'Dance with me Briony?'

Now she really must be dreaming, Briony thought as she circled the tiny floor in Ford's arms. Eyes closed she breathed in the scent of him, took pleasure from the quiet intimacy of their closeness. After a few minutes both his hands went to her waist and she slid her arms over his shoulders as if it was the most natural thing in the world. The band played 'Bewitched, Bothered and Bewildered' and Briony smiled at its appropriateness.

'Why are you smiling?' Ford asked as he lifted his head a fraction to look at her.

'Just—the song.' Her gaze locked with his.

'Are you bewitched, bothered and bewildered?'

'Mostly bewildered.'

'That's understandable,' he said dryly, 'I've been bewildered myself lately. And bothered,' his voice dropped to a whisper, 'and bewitched——'

His arms tightened around her, moulding her against

him and Briony hoped he wouldn't feel or hear the
bongo beat of her heart as it jumped about. A change in
the music tempo quickened their steps.

'Bongo drums,' Ford murmured and Briony drew
back sharply.

'What?'

'You don't hear them much these days,' he said
eyeing her flushed countenance.

'Oh no,' she agreed in relief as she heard the genuine
article in the band. Most people probably didn't!

Her eyes went to the dais. Over Ford's shoulder she
caught the eye of one of the musicians. He was smiling
at her—smirking. Her eyes opened a little wider. It was
Duane. Gone was the lank-haired youth clad in devil's
black. Here was a lean, attractive young man in elegant
clothes. But the smirk was the same and Briony knew a
stab of unease that his resident band job should be here.
And of disbelief. Explosive Duane in this serene setting.
Ford felt her tension and loosened his hold. 'Something
wrong?'

She shook her head and minutes later they went back
to their table. Away from Duane's stare, she saw how
foolish it was to let him bother her. Even so, she was
glad when Ford signalled for the bill and they drank
their coffee to leave.

They were almost to the door when Duane appeared
beside them.

'Briony, sweetheart,' he said and took her shoulders.

'Hello Duane,' she made a small, determined tug
against him but he held her.

'You look gorgeous.' Malice shone in his eyes and he
said just loud enough for her to hear, 'We are aiming
high darling. His Lordship won't mind a kiss from an
old friend I hope?' He bent his newly groomed head and
planted a quick, hard kiss on her mouth before she
could turn away. 'Ah, its been a long time,' he sighed as
if he was referring to the kiss. 'Drop in one day for a
drink—for old time's sake, sweetheart. You know
where I am.'

With a look of triumph he was gone, nodding
cheerfully at Ford's expressionless face. Briony was left

standing—shivering at the cold front that rushed to engulf her. 'I don't know where he lives' she wanted to say and, 'We've never been close the way he was pretending,' but the words remained unsaid.

Ford took her arm and they went to the car.

'A friend of yours?' he queried with a sardonic twist to his mouth and she saw her dream shattering to pieces. Damn, damn—she cursed inwardly and anger filled her. Anger that Duane should need to mend his fragile ego by such a stupid gesture—anger that she must always be explaining herself to Ford.

'Yes,' she snapped as he started the engine. 'Another boyfriend. I've got hundreds, Ford, didn't you know? Or is it thousands? I just haven't counted lately.'

It was almost twenty minutes before he spoke again. 'I don't intend to cross examine you about every man you've known Briony.'

'How awfully kind of you,' she flung at him, stung by the condescending tone and that 'every man'. 'It wouldn't take long if you did.'

'But in future I'd appreciate it if you'd avoid the embraces of old flames when you're out with me.'

She flared at the dry arrogance of his tone. 'Oh you would, would you? Well don't think that I——' His words hit her properly' 'In future'? 'When you're out with me'? 'What do you mean—in future?'

'Just that.'

'Oh.' There was a rush of music inside her head, a flurry of drums.

'Does that mean you don't care about them?' she ventured thinking how little there was for him to be jealous about—if he was jealous.

'No it doesn't mean that,' he told her impatiently. 'When I think of you with other—— No. But my own past is not exactly free of entanglements and it would be hypocritical of me to expect yours to be.'

His generosity annoyed her. Only because it was unnecessary. Suddenly Briony saw the humour of it. Ford was behaving in a very civilised fashion—the modern man confronted with the liberated woman.

How very big of him to waive her previous lovers. To grant her the right to have had them.

He put the radio on and they drove to its music for more than an hour. Dreamy music, romantic strings and gentle bossa nova rhythms. Briony put her head back and smiled a little into the darkness. There would be a way to tell him that there wasn't and never had been—anyone else in her life. But that 'in future' was enough to be going on with at the moment. She closed her eyes, dreaming and conscious of Ford just an arm's length away. When the car slowed, she sat up in time to see the pillars of Abingdon sweep past. The headlights shone on the long, curving drive down which she'd run from him once in her high heeled boots.

'It's early,' he said as he parked beside the house. 'So I thought we'd have a drink while we listen to some music I think you'll like.'

As they went up the steps, Briony hoped the music he had in mind went well with bongo drums, for her own personal band of them had struck up again.

Inside the study, Briony could almost hear the ghostly sound of the carousel again. The lamp threw its glow over the room's lush textures and her senses sharpened with her awareness of that first time here. He switched on a wall heater and some music, took her jacket and went out. Briony wandered to the book shelves and this time saw the name on one of the trophies. 'S. BARRON'. She smiled. So it wouldn't have given her the clue anyway. Amy had never mentioned 'Barron'. Her clue had been the twin apprehension at meeting 'Barry Ford' again, and passing inspection by Stanford. It had been one and the same thing.

Ford came back in and put an ice bucket down. He had removed his jacket and tie and unbuttoned his shirt at the neck.

'Sorry—no soup,' he smiled at her.

'Cor blimey guv—no soup yer say? Ain't much to arsk.'

He chuckled as he mixed two drinks and brought them to the chesterfield.

'You do that rather well. My first thought when I heard you was "how the hell can I put up with that accent".' Sitting down next to her, he slid one arm along the back of the settee.

'But you didn't know then that you'd ever see me again.'

'I would have found a way,' he said quite simply and Briony looked at him startled, and was caught in the trap of his gaze. Without taking his eyes from her, he put his drink down on the table, removed hers from unresisting fingers. All his cool reserve had fled. Ford's blue eyes were warm—the thin mouth parted and sensual. He stood and took her hand gently, then as if patience had worn thin, he catapulted her into his arms.

'These last weeks have been murder,' he whispered against her mouth, 'I've never stopped wanting you.' His kiss was fierce, forcing open her lips with bruising hunger while his hands roamed hard and urgent over her body. Briony felt the zip of her dress slide apart and the touch of his hand on her skin. Then her bra fastening was swept aside and his hands were curving about her bare breasts and his head was bending ... Briony trembled with the sensation but she began to be afraid. She had no illusions that she could set him at arm's length like the last time. There would be no turning back, but his fire outstripped hers and she needed time to match him. It was all too fast.

'Ford—I want——' she gasped as his tongue tipped the nipple of one breast.

'So do I, my love,' he breathed and took her lips again, peeling down the dress so that it dropped to her hips and she was all but naked in his arms.

'Ford,' she whispered, drowning, 'It's the first time——'

He put a finger over her mouth. 'No need to say that Briony. I'm not such a chauvinist that I have to be the first. I thought I made that clear. I'd like to be—but it doesn't matter.' He picked her up and began to walk, bending to kiss her again.

It mattered to her.

She had waited for this and somehow he had to

know—this one and only first time. It was there in her eyes—the plea to be believed now when it was more important than ever. He saw it and drew back.

'Briony?'

'Ford, I want to stay with you, but I've never done this——'

He blinked, stood there with her in his arms.

'Never?' he repeated as if it was something new and amazing to consider. She shook her head. 'Twenty-two and all those years playing with a band and you haven't had an affair?' he said and the faint thread of amusement surprised and angered her, even though his voice was gentle with belief.

'No—I haven't.' She turned a bright red. 'Sorry about that—I know I'm slow for my age and could have had numerous——'

His mouth silenced her, took her protests and embarrassment and turned them into flaring response. Her arms wrapped tight about his neck and her lips moved urgently against his. Now that he knew, she had no qualms. This was what she had been heading for since first she'd woken in his arms in this room with the carousel playing ourside. She could almost hear the song . . . '. . . the loveliest night of the year. . .'.

Ford put her down and her feet touched the floor reluctantly.

'Stuart's right,' he murmured as he adjusted her dress, zipped it up. 'I'm a fool.' His lips brushed hers gently and his hands settled on her waist, holding her close against him. 'I want you Briony, but we'll take it at your pace.'

'Ford—I'll stay with you——' she began and almost wilted under the intensity of the gaze he turned on her.

'That's an offer I don't want to refuse, believe me,' he smiled. 'But a girl deserves a little wooing for her debut. I'll take you home.'

He held her hand as they walked from his car to her caravan. 'I'll come over to see you tomorrow afternoon,' he told her and she nodded. 'Keep the evening free for me.' She nodded again, bursting with feelings and no words for them. The simple pressure of

his hand over hers almost choked her with love. He had
recognised and understood her apprehension and put
aside his own fiery need. This was a man she had waited
for. A tiny laugh escaped her and she swung her arm a
little, feeling the weight of his in their clasped hands.

'Share the joke?'

'No joke. I was just thinking how marvellous
everything is.' Words of declaration hovered on her
tongue but she caught them back. 'The moon—and the
stars——' she went on foolishly. 'See how they shine in
the pool.'

'Lovely,' he said gravely. 'And the sheen on the
cabana roof—see how the moon highlights the metal
ribbing.'

'Metal ribbing?' she repeated, 'Have you no romance
in your soul?'

Ford caught her up in his arms. 'Yes, I have,' he
whispered into her hair and somehow his mouth
wandered to hers and the night of moon and stars spun
about Briony. As the kiss deepened, the stars whirled
faster—she was on the carousel and turning, turning
and she never wanted to step off. 'Let me see you to
your door.' Ford let her go and took her hand again.
Their reflections followed them along the edge of the
pool until they skirted the cabana. She found her key
and Ford opened the door, then leaned one shoulder
against the metal of the van.

'In you go—and quickly,' he urged in a low voice.
'Should you hear a splash before I leave it will be me—
swimming.'

'Swimming?'

'The next best thing to a cold shower,' he grinned.

She scurried up the steps and his laughter, rich and
deep echoed back across the water as he left. And she
laughed too at the querulous croak of the frog.

She stretched awake in the morning, happiness
bubbling up in her even before she identified its source.

'I love you,' she mumbled to the pillow, then jumped
from bed hugging it to her.

'I love you——' she giggled at the lush prayer plant
with its new leaf, '—and you——' to the guitar that

glowed honey in the early morning sun slanting in. She threw down the pillow and flung open the door. The sound of Victor's trilling came faintly from the big house.

'And you Victor,' she called, 'I love you too.'

'Well, well—fair bursting with it this morning, aren't we?' George ambled into the annexe, the smell of his tobacco preceding him.

'George!' Briony flushed, still posed in her pyjamas at the top of the van steps with her arms outflung. She must look about to take a cue in a musical. 'I didn't think anyone was around.'

'Thought not. Didn't know you were so attached to that canary.' His eyes sparkled at her as he pulled complacently on his pipe. She grinned, unable to hold back the joy that spilled from her.

'Oh sure—I adore Victor.'

'Hmm. Must have had a good day in the city yesterday. A few weeks back you looked like a stunned mullet.'

'A stunned mullet?' Briony giggled. 'George, have you ever seen a stunned mullet?'

'Course I have. It looked just like you did after that parachuting business and before that, Ford's party. Might have had something to do with your falling in the pool that night of course.'

'Amy told you?'

'Hmmm. Said you'd lost some pendant thing of hers before Ford pulled you out or some such thing.'

'Yes,' Briony sobered. 'I can't think what happened to it. I've told Amy she can take the cost out of my wages.'

'Well now—was it gold with a green stone?'

'Yes, but——'

'Like this?' He pulled the gold chain from his pocket and Briony fell on it with a screech of delight.

'Stopped to see if grubs had got into Amy's potted palms out there by the pool and found it in the one that's sharing space with geraniums. Picked off a few dead leaves and there it was.'

'George, you marvellous man.' She kissed him on the cheek.

'I know, I know,' he said modestly and went on, 'Amy must be sleeping late today. I knocked but there's no answer. She's usually an early bird like me. Is she all right do you thinks Briony? She's looking a bit tired lately.'

'She was a bit weary from shopping, George, but okay. The Walters' invited her to stay in town overnight to see the *Mikado*. Her goddaughter is driving her back this morning.'

'Ah,' was all that George said but he eyed her through his screen of blue-grey smoke. 'Came back by train did you?'

'No.' She avoided his glance and held up the pendant to the light. 'This was all I needed, George. Now I've found Amy's jewel and I've . . .' a small smile curved her mouth.

'Discovered this affection for Victor?' he prompted when she stopped. 'Trouble with that kind of bird is—it sings so sweetly you can begin to think it has an attachment for you.'

The emerald swung from her fingers. 'He likes me George.'

'No doubt. Selfish things, canaries. Get so used to having people give them what they want—still there's always the exception.'

'Yes.' Briony moved the emerald and it winked as she brushed off the clinging dirt. 'Used to people giving them what they want . . .' there were no words of love between her and Ford. 'I want you' he'd said from the start and he was prepared to bide his time to have what he wanted.

George got up to go. 'Just remember what I told you about canaries. You can get too attached to the damned things and then they just fly away.'

Technically speaking it was her day off, but Briony was digging in the front garden when Amy came home. The rich, damp smell of earth rose to her and made pleasure of what should have been a chore. The sun was warmer as the last few days of winter merged into spring. A few clouds clung on the horizon but as yet the morning sun rose higher in an otherwise blue sky. With the spade in the earth, Briony stood and leaned on it, breathing in the tranquillity, conscious of a tiny caterpillar of doubt nibbling away at the happiness she'd woken with.

Sandalwood Street's peace was shattered as a sports car shrieked into it and tore to a stop. When Amy got out, helped by a petite, auburn-haired girl, Briony wiped her hands on her jeans and clumped towards them, a grimy, perspiring figure in her T-shirt, jeans and rubber boots.

'Briony—this is Maree, my goddaughter.'

The girl smiled and her silky smooth hair bobbed around her ears. She was wearing baggy pants and a top sashed at the waist and the whole outfit screamed a famous designer's name and oodles of money. Briony felt like a country clod by comparison.

'Hi.' Maree dumped a few of Amy's parcels into Briony's arms and she swallowed a flash of resentment. After all she was the odd-job girl.

'Did Stanford see you home all right last night my dear?' Amy enquired as they paused at the door for her to use her keys.

'Oh yes,' she ducked her head behind the pile of packets in her arms and was aware of Maree's instant attention.

'Oh goodie,' she exclaimed, 'Is Fordie down for the weekend? I'll go over and see him, talk him into taking me to lunch.'

Briony left them together and walked into Stocklea for a few groceries before the shops closed. The natty sports model had gone from the kerb when she came back. No doubt, Briony thought as she put her groceries away, Maree would be at Abingdon, fluttering her pansy eyes at 'Fordie' in effective persuasion. She couldn't imagine him refusing to take Maree somewhere special for lunch. Maree would talk his language—the language of those from the same background. Maree was the kind of girl who married people like Ford and was an asset at all those cocktail parties where she would be old schoolfriends with the girls who married other people like Ford. The cupboard doors banged. She roughly pushed aside the pot plant that had received her loving salute only hours earlier and sat down to eat lunch.

'I'm jealous,' she thought, 'and for no reason at all.' The girl knew him. That was all she could assume. 'Sorry,' she said to the pot plant and returned it to its position of prominence with a penitent stroke of the leaves.

But Amy went to golf and returned and Ford did not come as he'd promised. Briony had no difficulty in imagining him and Maree at a table for two in a country hotel, laughing with each other over their excellent wine.

Amy was ecstatic about the *Mikado*. Briony looked closely at her as she chattered. 'My dear the cleverest man played Koko. . . .' Was it her imagination or did the old lady look a trifle drawn?

'You look tired Amy—are you okay?'

'Of course, of course,' she replied with a touch of irritation and Briony dared not say more.

It was later, after dinner, that she remembered she still had not returned the pendant. As she took the silver slides from her hair and dropped them into her jewel box, the emerald shone up at her, incongruous with her few trinkets. Her forgetfulness about it was a fair indication of her mental state, she reflected. Never had she been so negligent where someone else's property was concerned. The sound of a car, followed by laughter at the house stopped her from going up with it. Amy's card-playing guests had arrived. Tomorrow she would take it back. George would be one of the party and no doubt would tell Amy it was safe for tonight anyway.

The wind sprang up and rattled the old pods on the cassia until it sounded like rain. Dressed in an old, old cheesecloth dress that flapped around her ankles, Briony mooned about, watching the tiny wrinkles driven across the pool's surface by the wind, kneeling to inspect her garden bed in the pale light from the van. Her seeds had sprouted in tiny buds of baby green. After a while she switched off the van's light and took her guitar into the annexe to play by the soft radiance that reached her from the light by the pool. The wind was tamed by the annexe walls, but enough entered to lift her hair about her shoulders and cut coolly through the open weave of her dress. But she stayed there, running through her classical repertoire and the melancholy lament of a Spanish song. Another car stopped outside the house and Briony heard the door slam as she let her hands drop from the strings. More voices and laughter came and the pianola briefly played 'Black and White Rag'. Briony felt suddenly alone and on the outside. She pictured Ford with Maree's sleek head at his shoulder, moving on from a protracted lunch to a dinner for two. What a fool, she thought, ever to imagine she could be anything but on the outside. Irritated by her self-pity she gripped the guitar and strummed out a strident rock rhythm. It was one of the songs Silverhero had played that night before she'd grown to love this place. And Ford.

The noise of her playing was swept away as the wind bustled into the annexe and out again, taking the last chord's vibration with it. And he was there. Looking down at her with a smile on his tanned face that had the colour rushing to hers.

'Hi,' she said as casually as she could.

'I'm sorry I couldn't come sooner as I said,' he sat down opposite, 'I was a bit tied up this afternoon. I phoned but Amy didn't answer.'

Tied up was he? She thought of the petite Maree and it hurt. 'Business?' she enquired, 'On your weekend off?'

'I'm afraid so.'

Her fingers tightened on the neck of the guitar. How very easily he lied. How convincingly. If she hadn't seen the pansy-eyed Maree herself, anxious to beard him in his den, she would be sympathising with him for overwork.

'You must be awfully tired.' She leaned forward and gave him a burst of sympathy. 'All that close work you do must make you very tense.'

His eyes narrowed on her and his lips thinned. 'All right. What is it?'

Hazel eyes opened wide at him. 'Why what could it be, Fordie?' She wished the words recalled at once but it was too late.

He laughed shortly, '"Fordie"—what the devil——?'

Comprehension dawned and he laughed again. 'You mean Maree.' In one stride he was out of his chair and lifting her from hers, guitar and all. The blue eyes were bright with pleasure. 'You're jealous aren't you?'

His arms locked about her, pulling her hard against him and the guitar gave a muted twang as her wavering hand lowered it to brush against his leg. The touch of his mouth was fierce, compelling and Briony closed her eyes and drowned again as it mellowed into sensuous persuasion. In slow torment his lips moved to her temple then to her ear.

'Maree only stayed a half hour—I've been negotiating on the phone most of the day over something that came up.' His mouth twitched in amusement as he studied her dazed face. One hand came up to remove a strand of hair that flipped across her eyes in the breeze.

'Why didn't you tell me you slept in the Railway Station that night?' he asked softly and her eyes widened.

'George!'

'He told me tonight. Why did you let me think you were with someone?'

'Pride. And you didn't have to think that.'

His blue eyes acknowledged the thrust. 'You're right. I didn't have to. I've grown cynical—and now jealous. You know the feeling.'

There wasn't much point in denying it. 'Yes,' she nodded, 'I know the feeling—that day you kissed Elizabeth——'

'Good,' he said. 'She did it for the camera—I did it to get at you——' His mouth met hers softly, a touch so slight she barely felt it—a touch so intimate that her whole body flamed. Seconds, minutes, hours passed. He lifted his head and she reeled. No—only seconds.

'George threw out a few hints to me tonight. He looks on you as a daughter I think. At any rate he asked me what my intentions were.'

'You didn't shock him by telling him, I hope?' she said lightly, dismissing the pang of regret in her heart. For she had made up her mind to accept second best if that was all he offered. Love and marriage she could dream about forever, but Ford was here and now and at least she could bring her love to whatever relationship he had in mind.

'No. I didn't tell him,' he grinned. 'But it wouldn't necessarily shock him.'

It would, she thought. And Amy too. It would have shocked me once, she thought.

'It must have been hellish uncomfortable in that Ladies' Room.'

'The bench was a bit Spartan.'

'I was a bastard to you that night.'

'Oh, well—not really——'

'I was rough with you.'

'Perhaps a little——'

'A lot.'

'Would you like that right to the jaw now?'

He pointed to his chin. 'Right there.'

'No, I can't, because you were thoughtful too. You gave me your jacket to wear. Did you find it the next day?'

'That night. I put on the garden light, hoping to find you and there was my coat, neatly over the chair like a nicely phrased statement.'

'Of what?'

'Of thanks.'

'Well, that's promising. I was wishing I'd said thank you properly when I put it there. Our communications seem quite good.'

'Definitely.' Ford put his mouth to her ear, rubbed his lips along the soft, pale skin of her neck. 'For instance, I'm sure you know what I want right now, more than anything. . . .'

'I—I——' she stammered, thrown by the change from banter to husky passion.

'Exactly right,' he raised his head and grinned. 'So you will sing for me?'

The guitar twanged once more as she reached up to kiss him. Then she sang for him.

CHAPTER TEN

SUNDAY was dreary. It rained all morning until the pool level raised to the flagstones and Briony got out the manual to find out how to drain off the excess. She did some washing, using the drier for the first time since she had been here and curled up on her bed with the book she had bought in town. But her mind wasn't on the story and finally she put it down and stretched out to listen to the applause of the raindrops on the metal roof of the van. What a beautiful sound, she thought and a smile curved her mouth. What a beautiful world. What a beautiful man.

A knock at her door sent her flying to the mirror to drag the brush through her hair and tuck her shirt into the waistband of her jeans. She opened the door to a bearded, beaming man and it took her a few moments to recognise Mike and cover the stab of disappointment with welcoming noises. He shed his jacket in the annexe and came in, looking around and asking how she liked her new life.

'You've lost that lean and hungry look,' he teased, then went on to give her the latest news on Silverhero. 'I'm on my way to join the others at Goulburn after I've called in to see the folks at Moss Vale. Then it's the road to Gundegai.'

'And beautiful Wagga Wagga,' she grinned and he nodded.

'Yep. All that. And there won't be much snow left by the time we get back to the Snowy—well, I can't ski anyway.' He felt in his pockets. 'Jeff said if I called in to give you his spare key. Seemed to think you might get tired of gardening.'

'Tell him thanks,' Briony took the key. 'I don't think I'll be needing it. You can take his jacket back for me. I've had it since the Gala night. He might want it in the Snowy Mountains even if it is out of the ski season.'

She fetched the plaid jacket which she wrapped in brown paper and Mike tucked it under one arm. The rain had eased so she walked with him to the overloaded station sedan.

'Take care of yourself, Briony,' he grinned.

'You too. Give Jeff my love.' She touched a kiss to Mike's hairy cheek and he briefly hugged her. Then he tossed the parcel on to the passenger seat and eased his bulk inside.

'Say—isn't that the fellow who ran the Gala fête——?' he asked and Briony turned to see Ford getting out of his car. Mike looked a bit more closely at her flag red cheeks and suddenly bright eyes.

'Yes. He's Mrs Gordon's nephew.'

'Well, well. Small world.' Mike gave her a cheerful wave and drove off. Ford stood for a moment, watching him leave, then moved towards the house, not even the faintest smile in evidence.

'Good morning Briony,' was all he said as he stepped up the front path to the wide verandah. His polite indifference pulled her up, froze the soft words of welcome on her tongue. The rain began to fall again but she stood there for perhaps a minute after he'd gone inside, feeling a new cold inside that had nothing to do with the sting of raindrops on her skin. At last she was driven to her van by the weather. 'Good morning' from the man who had kissed her last night, called her 'my love'? 'Good morning' as if she was a mere acquaintance? Why?

Mike. Of course, that was it. He must have seen Mike's arm about her while she kissed him. What else could have brought the frown back to his brow and the harsh set to his mouth? She grabbed a hand towel and dried her hair, smoothing it back into a knot.

'It's not going to work,' she muttered and looked at herself in the mirror. Her hazel eyes were wide and hurting with the knowledge. She couldn't take this up-and-down emotional ride. Ford smiled—and her world was a palace. Ford frowned and it fell about her.

It rained harder, the noise a tattoo on the roof. What a rotten day, she thought and put her hands over her ears. Briony picked up the bestseller again but its words made no sense. Was it just Mike, she kept thinking. Could there be any other reason why he had looked straight through her?

One way to find out. Ask him. Briony firmed her mouth, took another look in the mirror to find her drying hair wisping about her face. She opened her jewel box and took a couple of slides to secure it and remembered the pendant. It was the ideal excuse to go up to the house and see Ford in the process. Where, she wondered had she put the box that Amy had given her with it? As she pondered, her mind refusing to budge from Ford, the emerald swung like a pendulum from her hand. Then she heard footsteps outside.

Warmth spread through her. He had come to see her after all. It would be all right. But it wasn't Ford whose head appeared in the doorway. It was Margot Drewett. She peered inside as if she expected to find someone else there too.

'I wanted to see you first before I went up to the house,' she said. 'To make sure you were still on the scene. You haven't been quite as clever as you thought, Miss Wilde. I told Aunt Amy she was a fool to hire you and it seems I was right . . .' she saw the emerald and her eyes glittered triumphantly. 'So you did have it all the time, you little——' She came inside, dripping water from an umbrella and snatched the chain from Briony. 'Well, things looked bad for you before but this proves how right I was. Maybe now Aunt Amy will listen to me.'

'I don't know what you're talking about,' Briony backed away from the malice in the other woman.

'They all say that though, don't they?' Margot went down the steps and looked back. 'What did you do with Aunt Amy's etching? And the Chinese figurine? I suppose some of your friends in the band know where to get rid of stolen property.'

'What etching? What figurine?'

'Oh dear. You're going to have to do better than that dear, when I show Aunt this.' She indicated the pendant and made a dash out into the rain, opening the umbrella as she ran.

'Stolen property' . . . the words rang in Briony's head. Was that why Ford was here now? 'If there is an item of my aunt's missing at any time I'll have you and your scruffy friends in custody . . .' Ford had said to her right at the beginning. Briony felt a chill fear. He had looked so stony . . . but surely he wouldn't believe she could steal from Amy. Not any more. No. It was something else . . . please let it be something else, she whispered and took her yellow raincoat. Holding it over her, she ran around the pool to the house. At least the pendant was not incriminating as Margot liked to think. George had found it and he would have told Amy so last night. By the time she knocked at the back door her confidence was returning. There was a mistake, no doubt embroidered upon by Margot who had never forgiven her for humiliating her lamb. All the same . . . she frowned, a theft in Amy's house?

Ford answered the door. 'What are you doing here?' he snapped and the colour drained from her face. 'Go back to your van Briony. I was coming down to see you anyway.' His grip on her arm was hard as he turned her to the steps, almost pushing her out. So he did believe it. Briony's chin trembled ominously. He didn't even want her in the house.

'I want to see Amy,' she gulped and wiped away the raindrops that ran down her face. 'And I'm not going until I do.' She broke free and went in.

Amy's tired, grey face was a physical blow to Briony. The old lady, for the first time since she'd known her, looked old. The lines on her face were pressed deep, the flesh between sagging as if all her optimism had fled and let it drop.

'My dear, I phoned Ford to come over to handle. . . .' Amy began when she saw her and her lined face looked more distressed than ever.

'Were you intending to sell the pendant too? Or just keep it?' Margot broke in, 'It's bad luck for you dear, that we found out so soon. Very smart to steal from that cabinet. It's so crowded that one or two things would never be noticed. If Gary hadn't wanted to borrow the etching of the old courthouse for his school's centenary, Amy might not have gone to it at all for months.'

'But I didn't take anything. Amy—I swear—and the pendant——'

'Very touching. But we've heard your innocent little act about the pendant. "Oh I can't think where I left it," and you had it all the time—were gloating over it.'

'Just a moment, Margot. Briony my dear,' Amy's voice at least seemed to have a vestige of warmth in it. 'We found this in the cabinet—and I think you know what that means——' She held up something and Briony went to look. It was a long, silver slide. Like the ones she wore constantly to keep her hair from her face while she worked. Exactly like the ones she wore now.

'It looks like one of mine,' she said quietly and looked at Ford. His face could have been carved from stone except for the muscle moving grimly in one cheek. He couldn't believe something as obvious as this—he couldn't.

'Perhaps you could tell us, Briony, if there's been any——' Amy began, but Ford cut in, his words as cold as the rain slicing down on the roof.

'There's no need for her to tell us a thing, Amy.' His mouth was a thin, angry line as he turned to Briony. 'Go back to your caravan and wait for me there,' he said curtly and strode from the house. They all heard the sound of his car door slam above the steady sound of the rain and the tyres shriek as he flung the vehicle from the kerb.

She didn't wait to think where he might be going. Hardly heard Margot's last spiteful gibe and Amy's sharp, 'Margot, don't make a fool of yourself.'

Tears rained down her face and she turned to run back through the house, barely finding her way through the sunroom jungle as she ran outside. She had a mental picture of Mike getting into his station sedan with a parcel—and Ford watching with the knowledge of the theft on his mind.

The pool was alive with a thousand dancing droplets, the flagstones awash and she almost fell in her blind haste, clutching at one of Amy's worn statues to save herself. Past the cabana and the drum of rain on its metal roof she ran and stopped, sobs dragging at her throat, in the annexe. Water ran from her hair and the yellow raincoat which she had clutched about her, and it was several minutes before she could think again.

She had to leave. Staying here to face Ford's harsh accusations would be unbearable. To go was unbearable. But there was no alternative. The rain came down in a solid sheet, bowing her head as she went to fetch her luggage from the cabana storeroom. Her tears had stopped. As she began to pack all the happy days of her life here into suitcases, she was dry-eyed and desolate. Not crying. The weather was doing that for her.

'Lovely weather for ducks,' a cheerful voice said from the annexe. 'I saw Margot's car outside. Can I stay here until she's gone?' George put his sou'westered head into the doorway, saw the suitcase and his smile disappeared. 'Not leaving, Briony, love, are you?'

'Come in, George. Yes—I'm afraid I have to go.'

George shrugged off his raincoat and left it outside. His hand went exploringly to his bulky shirt pocket, but he didn't take out the pipe. 'Why love?'

'As they say in the movies, George—I've been framed.' The carefully light tone of her voice failed— the last word came out shakily. 'Some things of Amy's are missing—and I, with my unsavoury past and shady friends, am the prime suspect. But I didn't take anything, George.'

'Of course you didn't,' he grunted, his hand patting his pocket in silent agitation. He put a few questions to her and mulled over the answers.

'So young Gary wanted it for his school, eh?' and, 'Ford cleared out, did he?'

He watched her jam a case closed. 'Did he tell you I had a word with him last night?'

She nodded, the tears springing up again.

'Asked him what he wanted with you—didn't seem at all clear to my mind . . . good thing if you ask me, if you went away before you—— Where are you going?'

'Back to Sydney I guess,' she sniffed and took the handkerchief that George offered to mop her eyes.

'No trains through Stocklea today. There's one from Bowral though. I'll drive you there in Amy's car.'

She had the keys, left trustingly in her care by Amy. Her shoulders shook again at the idea of leaving the old lady and George—and Ford. George transferred her luggage to the car, his sou'wester pulled low over the worried frown on his brow.

'We'll miss you, Briony, love,' he said. 'But it might be for the best.'

A last time she looked around the empty caravan. There was just the pendant's box and the prayer plant on the table on its cane planter. She touched the new leaf and looked at George.

'Would you take it?'

He nodded. 'I'll look after it for you love. Even talk to it if you like. . . .'

As George drove out, the rain sleeted down. Amy's house was a pale, silver outline behind it, the massive old fig tree with its budding spring growth, a twisted ghost.

The train clacked slowly into the maze of Sydney's tracks and Briony sat frozen. So much for dreams, she thought. So much for love and trust and a man who had smiled at her last night as if he might learn to love her. A wry smile twisted her mouth. A silver hairpin in the treasures cabinet! How obvious could you get? Stuart had warned her about spiders in her bed, frogs in her gumboots, but even he had not realised the sly sophistication of the Drewett boys. 'Gary wanted the etching for his school's centenary——' The spoiled boy had actually directed the scene from off-stage and been smart enough to dodge a personal appearance. The footprint in her garden was the only clue she'd had. And that had faded—was washed away long before the rain came.

But there had been the emerald. Her eyes closed in silent pain as she remembered Amy's tired, disillusioned face. George couldn't have told her that he'd discovered it. But he would soon and the old lady would know that she hadn't lied to her about that. And Ford would hear about it too . . . but it would make no difference.

He was not for her. How stupid of her to ever think he could be. She'd lost Amy and George. But Ford had never been hers to lose. Tears brimmed over just when she thought she'd cried them out. Now and then during the long trip, she'd sheltered behind her sunglasses and sniffed into George's handkerchief. Dear George, she thought, folding the sodden piece of cloth for a final sniff before the train stopped. He had been so comforting as he'd driven her to the station. Asked her if she had enough money—what she would do for work—whether she would play at that coffee lounge place again—asked several times where she would stay. But she hadn't told him that. She'd felt for Jeff's key in her pocket and merely said, 'I'll find a place.'

'You write to us—Amy and me—promise me that,' he'd said at the last. 'No matter what you think, Amy wouldn't believe all that rubbish—you let us know where you are, won't you?'

She would write—she'd promised that. But not to let them know where she was. Not that. She wanted to be safe from flame-blue eyes that gave her false hopes only to dash them to the ground. She didn't want to see Ford Barron again.

And she did not. Two days later she ate breakfast in Jeff's flat and looked through the Situations Vacant. It was almost as if she was right back to square one. As if she'd never seen an advertisement that said 'Quiet, restful surroundings——', never dreamed of fresh country air and the smell of new-mown grass. Never met a man who could turn her life upside down with a glance.

Now there were no more bongo drums—no more ups and downs. Just downs. She was off the carousel and on solid, safe, dull, depressing ground. Only at night did she step on the hurdy-gurdy again—dreaming snatches of a past life ... running from him with the sound of horse's hooves in her ears; falling from the tree. Their reflections caught by moonlight in the pool—the slow fire of his love-making and the laughter she'd reached in his careful, untrusting eyes.

A few jobs looked promising. If by promising you

meant excellent wages, air-conditioned premises and a
staff tennis court. Briony jotted down the phone
numbers and went to ring for appointments in the
phone booth on the corner. Jeff's phone was dead—
disconnected by the sound of it, whether by design or
by failure to pay the bill she wasn't sure. Probably the
latter.

She made her calls and hesitated in the booth. At
Sandalwood Street, the caravan would be standing
empty, the lawn would be thickening ready for cutting
again, the pool would need a vacuum and more
chlorine after all the rain. Her eyes were far away and
she could almost smell the grass—hear the heavy quiet
and the buzz of insects.

As the traffic roared and a paper boy called on the
corner she dialled Amy's number, suddenly anxious to
know that she was well. Her grey, lined face lingered in
her memory and she pressed the receiver close to her ear
in apprehension. The old lady's voice was firm, clear
and Briony breathed a sigh of relief.

'Briony! Where are you? George told us eventually
that you were in Sydney, but whereabouts? We're all
worried about you. Why did you run off like that you
silly girl? I didn't believe you took anything for a
moment . . . Briony? Are you there?'

'Yes, Amy. I'm here,' she managed to say at last and
blew her nose hard. 'Which question shall I answer
first?' she said with a shaky laugh. How marvellous it
was to know that Amy didn't believe her a cheap little
thief.

'Just this one—was it Ford you ran from?'

When she didn't say anything Amy said, 'Well you've
answered that one. Do you love him, Briony?'

'I—I——'

'Sounds like a "yes" to me. You've misunderstood
him, Briony. Now my dear, just tell me where you are
so that he can. . . .'

No, Briony thought as her heart started jumping all
over the place again. She couldn't go through that
again. Just talking about Ford started the carousel
turning and she wasn't taking that ride any more.

'What's that, Amy? I can't hear you. Amy—I'll phone back sometime on a better line. Bye.'

Tony and Speranza Rocco were as good as their word. They did welcome her back to the coffee lounge with open arms.

'Briony—when you coming to play for us again?' Tony asked with his flashing smile when she called at the coffee shop.

'I'm out of work again Tony—any time you like.'

'Friday—okay? Some of the kids, they ask for you.'

'Really?' she smiled, genuinely pleased.

'One real nice man asked about you coming back,' Speranza gave her a sly look. 'Maybe the boyfriend you leave behind to go to the country?'

'What was he like?'

'Tall and a little bit—er—scruffy?'

'Scruffy.' Briony grinned. 'That sounds like Martin. I used to go out with him once.' When they'd broken up, he had said he would stay in touch. Martin's ego just hadn't been able to accept that he wasn't irresistible.

Speranza shook her head. 'You shouldn't have let that one go Briony—he's a real man.' She rolled her eyes at her husband, 'Like my Tony.'

Briony smiled as they ribbed her about Martin. He'd never seemed quite that impressive, but then the Rocco's dearly loved to find marriage prospects for her and any other single girl who crossed their paths.

'Friday then,' she said as she left.

'That's good. We give you some pizza—fatten you up for Martin.'

The flat seemed lonelier than ever after the Rocco's cheerful friendliness. In fact, Briony thought, as she dressed carefully and attended several interviews, the city, packed with people, was a lonely desert compared with Stocklea.

On Friday night she took her guitar and caught a bus to Rocco's with gratitude. At least there she would have the illusion of cosiness among the customers in the tiny dim lit place.

'Your Martin called in again last night,' Speranza whispered. 'He's crazy for you, that man.'

'Oh sure, I believe you,' Briony said grinning. 'You're not trying to play cupid are you Speranza?'

'Cupid?' the Italian woman looked surprised. 'No—no. I got the figure for it but not the aim.' Her plump body wobbled as she laughed. Briony went to her table in the corner and began to play.

The instant she touched the guitar strings, images of Ford flooded her mind. The last time she'd played had been for him, not quite a week ago. How incredible that she had almost been convinced then that Ford might grow to love her. Within a day those hopes had crashed around her.

The coffee lounge filled up and the buzz of voices and clink of cups drove out her wistfulness. Briony ran through her usual repertoire of standards, a few top forty numbers and stopped for coffee, delivered to the table by a perspiring Tony.

'That's nice,' he beamed. 'Gives our place class, lovely young lady playing nice, soft music. Maybe I put up the price of the coffee if you stay this time,' he went away, laughing.

In fact most people were laughing Briony noticed, as she sipped her coffee. Or at least smiling. It should have made her happy but it had the opposite effect. When she resumed playing, the music just wouldn't come out anything but blues. A few people actually clapped as she finished one song and Tony paused on his way to a table. 'Now I definitely put up the price,' he said in a stage whisper.

She riffled through her music folder, searching for something she hadn't played for a while but in the end she put it aside and played one that popped into her head—one that she knew would not be dimissed until she did so. 'I'm wild again—beguiled again——' she began to sing and heard this lovely song turning into a blues number too as it brought its associated memories of Ford . . . dancing close to him, her head pressed to his shoulder. His deep voice saying, 'Are you bewitched, bothered or bewildered?' Her eyes closed and she could almost feel his warmth, smell the tang of that after shave he used. For a moment her voice wobbled, but the words kept flowing from her and she opened her eyes wide to discourage her tears.

And saw him. Tall and broad-shouldered, tan and sombre—standing by the entrance, watching her. The last word of the song stayed in Briony's throat and she blinked at Ford's mirage. But when she looked again, the mirage was moving, weaving through the tables until it loomed over her.

'Where the hell have you been?' he growled and her hands trembled on the guitar.

'You're real,' she breathed. He sat down and ran a hand through his hair. It looked decidedly unlike his usual groomed style. It was scruffy and uncombed, as if he'd spent rather a lot of time running his hand through it. There were circles under his eyes that matched hers, and the frown line was sharp as a sword cut above his nose.

'Yes I'm real,' he snapped. 'I'll show you just how real as soon as I get you alone. What the devil do you mean by running away like that? I told you to wait for me in the caravan.'

'Oh,' she stiffened. 'And what made you think I would want to wait for you to come back, accusing me of thieving your aunt's treasures and—and conniving to keep her jewellery?'

He snorted impatiently. 'I didn't think that, you stupid girl. It was Margot's boys—I suspected as much right away—so did Amy.'

'But you were so angry with me before that—you didn't even smile at me outside in the garden and then when I came up to the house, you spoke to me as if. . . .'

Tony came over, a broad smile flashing, and took Ford's crisp order for some coffee. He winked at Briony as he left.

'Yes, I was blazing mad.' Ford admitted. 'But not the way you obviously thought. First I was eaten up with jealousy when I saw you kiss that hairy great brute in the street ... then I wanted to keep you out of Margot's reach while she was spitting accusations left, right and centre. I was so furious with her and those two little—monsters of hers, that it was all I could do to keep my hands from her neck.'

Briony hardly heard him after the first few words—'jealousy' she thought, and the bongo drums began again.

'Then you didn't believe I'd stolen anything? I thought when you saw Mike with that parcel——?'

'I might have thought it suspicious once. But no. Don't you know by now that I——' he broke off as Tony arrived with two coffees. He winked again.

'Did you come in here last night?' Briony asked suddenly, light dawning. 'Tall and scruffy' was a brand new description for Ford.

'Yes. And earlier in the week. And I phoned your damned brother's flat only to find the phone disconnected. Then I tracked down the band.'

'Silverhero?' she exclaimed. 'But they're on the road.'

'Don't I know it. I tried every Leagues Club, every R.S.L. from Goulburn to Gundegai down to Tumut.'

'How did you know they were touring there?'

'You told Stuart and Stuart told me—when I phoned him in Melbourne.'

Her eyes opened wide. 'You've gone to a lot of trouble to find me,' she said and her voice was low and husky. 'Did you finally speak to Jeff?'

'Yes. He said you were probably staying at his flat and gave me the address. I was going there next.'

'Jeff must have thought . . . what did he say?'

'He said—you must be Ford Barron, Mrs Whatsername's nephew. I don't know how he recognised my voice—I forgot to say who I was.'

'Mike must have told him you were related to Amy. And Jeff remembered your name?' Briony's head whirled. Jeff had guessed. She tried to think just what she had said to give herself away. But with Jeff it wouldn't have to be very much. And he'd remembered the name—the right name after all this time. If he'd done that at the start, she would have been forewarned, would have run again long before this to avoid Ford Barron. She began to feel like laughing—and crying.

'What did you say?'

Ford lifted his coffee and watched her over the rim of it as he sipped. 'I told him he'd better start calling me

Ford. And don't,' he added irritably as she opened her mouth, 'ask me what he said again.'

'I wasn't going to.' She lapsed into silence, wondering where they went from here. Ford drank his coffee and watched her saying nothing.

'Did George explain about the pendant?' she ventured.

He nodded.

'I left the box belonging to it in the van.'

'Yes, I found it on the table.' His face set black as thunder. 'And that was all I found. When I got back and saw your van was empty I very nearly——' He took a deep breath. 'I'd been to Margot's house to bring back those two damned little thugs and the etching and the figurine. A rare old scene, that was. Margot prostrate with outrage and accusing me of treason for putting the blame on her lambs until she saw the proof. And Amy, on her dignity as you've never seen her. The grand old lady, icily dressing down the boys and their mother until they felt like mere atoms.'

Briony could imagine it all too well. She had turned their well-ordered lives upside down, one way and another.

'And while I was busy clearing your name you ran out on me.'

'But I thought you didn't want me.'

He said a word she'd never expected to hear from him.

'My God, Briony if we were alone I swear I'd——'

'You'd what?' she enquired, a warmth welling up in her—a new kind of certainty.

He didn't answer, looked down at his empty cup.

'Everyone's warned me about hurting you. Amy—George—even Stuart in his roundabout way. What nobody seems to have considered is that you might hurt me.'

'Could I do that?' the words came out on the ghost of a breath.

'You will if you run away from me again.'

There was an outburst of laughter from a near-by table. The shoosh of the coffee machine as Speranza put a jug of milk under the steam pipe. Tony cheerfully took another order for raisin toast.

'I had a few warnings about you too,' she said. 'About your prowess with women—your irresistible line—your determination to have what you want.'

'That sounds like George. He said all that to me last week in our heart-to-heart. He's right of course.'

'What? Your prowess? Your irresistible line?'

'No about getting what I want.' His blue eyes were very bright as he leaned across the table and took her hand. 'I want you. For always. Marry me, Briony.'

'But I'm not sophisticated—I'm not a gracious hostess. You need someone like Elizabeth—or Maree.' Her pulses thundered in her ears, Why am I arguing? she thought.

'Can they play rock and roll and sing French ballads? Speak with a Cockney twang and fall out of trees and into pools?' he asked. 'You see I've discovered that I need someone like that. Someone to make me laugh and drive me insane.'

'Oh well—I can do that,' she laughed but there was a lump in her throat all the same. She would have to learn to die a little every time he trusted himself to a parachute. But she would do it. Had to.

His hand tightened on hers. 'I love you, Briony.'

'Oh, Ford, I fell in love with you long before I started falling out of trees and into the pool.'

'When?' he prompted.

'I'm supposed to ask that. It's always women who want to know——'

'When?'

'When I came out of that faint and felt your arm around me. You looked so stern but I think I fell for you then anyway.'

'I can do better than that,' he said.

'Oh?'

'First sight,' he nodded ruefully at her surprise. 'It serves me right to be bowled over by a comic strip heroine with a guitar. I've always been too much in control, too damned smug.'

'I know. George told me. You canaries are all the same.'

His eyebrows rose. 'You can explain that to me later.'

He leaned all the way across the table and kissed her on the lips, a hard, longing kiss that set the bongo drums in full spate.

'Thank God for that,' he said as they drew a few inches apart. 'I can't go back to Stocklea without a wedding date set. Amy is already checking her orchids for your bouquet and George mentioned something about a new suit when he saw me tearing about like a madman trying to find you.' He paused. 'I'm assuming your answer is yes.'

'Yes—yes—yes! I'm so lucky,' she looked at him with stars in her eyes. 'To have you—and all those marvellous people. Amy—George—your brother——'

'God, how I hated Stuart at that party—making you laugh with that easy manner of his. He was more your age and you had music in common. I began to think he might step in. He told me all that cuddling at the landing field that day was because you were worried about me.'

'I was,' she said. 'Stuart's like my brother to me. But you hated Neil too.'

He nodded wryly. 'A fleeting jealousy that. But he was just a kid. I wasn't really seriously worried by him.'

'You looked daggers at Duane.'

'Who's Duane?'

'The guitarist at the restaurant. He only pretended we'd been close to pay off an old score. I rebuffed him a few times with the band and bruised his ego. You wouldn't have recognised him. He used to play for Silverhero.'

Ford nodded gravely. 'I confess to a few doubts about him. But I'm not basically a jealous man.'

Briony snorted. 'Mike?'

'Ah—the hairy one. Yes, well—it did occur to me that——'

'Nothing,' she shook her head. 'Absolutely nothing. A big brother image entirely I assure you.'

'How many big brothers have you got?'

Her fingers curled into his hand and she raised her eyes in consideration. 'Well—I think that's about the lot.'

'It had better be.' Ford kissed her again, lingeringly, unheeding of the customers grinning at them. Tony came over to remove the coffee cups and sighed at them.

'Ah—it's nice. But now I'm gonna lose my guitar player again I suppose?'

Ford smiled. 'I'm afraid so.'

Tony slapped him on the back. 'Speranza and me— we both know you're crazy for her when you come in yesterday. Take care of her, Martin.' He loped off to Speranza's summons.

'Martin?' Ford repeated ominously.

'Oh. I can explain about Martin . . .' she giggled. 'I used to go out with Martin but he's——'

'Not another big brother?'

'Not anything. Ford,' she touched his face and was serious, 'there has been no-one and never will be anyone but you.'

He gripped her hand so hard that she grimaced.

'Good,' he replied in a voice made husky. 'Now let's go to my apartment. I have to propose properly to you.'

'It was a beautiful proposal.'

'But without frills,' he said his eyes warm with promise.

'I've never cared much for frills,' Briony told him breathlessly.

'You'll like these.' He smiled at her flushed face. 'Is this your guitar case?'

She nodded, bursting with happiness. 'Just one last song for Tony's customers before we go——' she managed a few bars of a familiar waltz before a large, tanned hand removed the guitar from her grasp. Another hand pulled her to her feet and held her close.

'There'll be no last song, Briony,' he whispered and kissed her.

They didn't hear the customers' applause. They were on the carousel and turning, turning. . . .

Coming Next Month in Harlequin Romances!

2689 DARK NIGHT DAWNING Stacy Absalom
An injured concert pianist hides her suspicions about the hit-and-run nightmare that destroyed her career and crippled her faith in her ex-fiancé... until he starts pursuing her again!

2690 STAG AT BAY Victoria Gordon
Following a disastrous marriage, a young widow retreats to her father's Queensland deer farm and tries to turn her back on men, especially her father's partner and his improbable dreams.

2691 A TIME TO GROW Claudia Jameson
A Yorkshire woman is no longer the difficult teenager her grandfather's protégé once rescued from one humiliating scrape after another. She's grown up and determined to be acknowledged as a woman.

2692 YEAR'S HAPPY ENDING Betty Neels
Is it a young nanny's destiny to settle into a permanent post caring for other people's children, or will an infuriatingly cynical widower be proven wrong?

2693 MAN AND WIFE Valerie Parv
Running her father's Australian property-development empire would be simpler if her home wasn't in such a mess. What she needs is a wife. What she gets is a man and a world of complications.

2694 BRIDE BY CONTRACT Margaret Rome
For a price — the ancestral home for her grandmother and employment for her disentitled brother — an English aristocrat agrees to marry a shrewd Canadian millionaire with an eye for bargains.

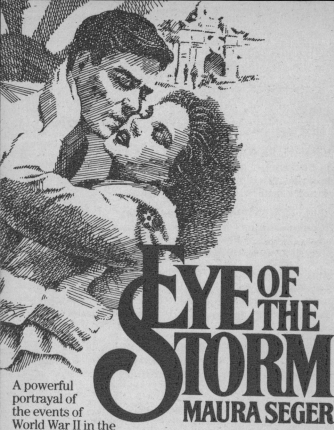

EYE OF THE STORM

MAURA SEGER

A powerful portrayal of the events of World War II in the Pacific, *Eye of the Storm* is a riveting story of how love triumphs over hatred. Aboard a ship steaming toward Corregidor, Army Lt. Maggie Lawrence meets Marine Sgt. Anthony Gargano. Despite military regulations against fraternization, they resolve to face together whatever lies ahead.... A searing novel by the author named by *Romantic Times* as 1984's Most Versatile Romance Author.

At your favorite bookstore in March or send your name, address and zip or postal code, along with a check or money order for $4.25 (includes 75¢ for postage and handling) payable to Harlequin Reader Service to:

In the U.S.
Box 52040
Phoenix, AZ 85072-2040

In Canada
5170 Yonge Street
P.O. Box 2800
Postal Station A
Willowdale, ONT   M2N 6J3

EYE-A-1